EVERYTHING
HAD BEEN WONDERFUL
UNTIL . . .

His jaw tightened as his eyes played over her torn dress in a way that made Gail turn pale. "What a fool I was to think you'd changed! It's the same scene as three years ago, isn't it? Only the faces are different."

His searing sarcasm made Gail stop clutching the torn remnants of her dress. She felt the nails bruise her palms instead. "So you did remember me? I thought you might . . ."

"My God, yes." He uttered a brief, mirthless laugh. "You're the kind of woman that's hard to forget, Miss Alden."

LOVE
IN
DANGER

Glenna Finley

A SIGNET BOOK from
NEW AMERICAN LIBRARY
TIMES MIRROR

SIGNET, SIGNET CLASSICS, MENTOR, PLUME AND MERIDIAN BOOKS
are published by The New American Library, Inc.,
1301 Avenue of the Americas, New York, New York 10019

FIRST PRINTING, JANUARY, 1973

5 6 7 8 9 10 11 12 13

PRINTED IN THE UNITED STATES OF AMERICA

Thou shouldst have looked before thou
hadst leaped.

—Jonson

CHAPTER ONE

The first classified ad in the Paris edition of the *New York Herald Tribune* was a dilly.

"WANTED: Discreet American woman with secretarial experience to supervise child in Portugal for two weeks. Generous salary. Only those with highest morals need apply. Write Box 15 by Tuesday latest."

That "highest morals" bit would make any woman choke, Gail Alden decided. It was a good thing the "generous salary" was mentioned first. She read the notice a second time and, for the moment, the noisy honking of Parisienne taxis and crowded sidewalks by the famed Café de la Paix blurred in the background.

Finished, she stared at the advertisement and wondered about the author's identity. Probably it was some Pilgrim Father who thought nursemaids should transcribe letters between blowing noses and scrubbing childish knees.

She shook her head. So her traveler's checks were getting thin . . . she still wasn't *that* desperate!

At the next table, an aging Frenchman ignored his aperitif to concentrate on her attractive figure. This wasn't unusual. From her coppery-brown hair styled casually short to deep blue eyes framed by thick lashes, Gail was enough to make any Frenchman stare. By the time his gaze had gone over her clear complexion, lingered on well-shaped lips, and finished with her small, straight nose buried so perversely in the newspaper, he decided it was time to improve Franco-American relations.

He cleared his throat noisily. This served only to attract the attention of the waiter who was impatiently waved away. *Mon Dieu!* Why must the American woman keep staring at that accursed newspaper? He watched her lips move and strained to hear the words.

"Discreet woman . . . high morals," Gail was murmuring. "What kind of a dum-dum would use expressions like that? He probably expects references from the Recording Angel!" She slapped the paper down with an exasperated grimace.

Her hopeful neighbor wilted when he saw that look. Some things needed no translating. He shifted sadly in his chair and decided to concentrate on easier prey—like the buxom brunette sitting two tables away.

Gail had missed the entire byplay. She rested her elbows on the metal table and took a sip of her bitter French coffee while the words from the "Help Wanted" column remained stubbornly in front of her eyes. Apart from the phrasing, the advertisement sounded like the very thing she had been hoping for.

Not that Gail had experienced much difficulty in behaving herself in the past twenty-four years. From high school on, her main trouble had been convincing men that just because her figure measured 35-24-34, it did not necessarily follow that her brain registered 0-0-0. It had taken four years and her recent promotion to Chief of Personnel for a large Cleveland pharmaceutical company to vindicate her efforts.

Unfortunately, nothing could have prevented her present difficulty. A sudden illness had prevented Sharon, her traveling companion, from joining her in Paris on the date planned and the prospect of three extra weeks in Europe's most expensive city already had Gail's vacation budget on the ropes.

She tucked the newspaper into her purse and chewed the edge of her lip. Beggars couldn't be choosers. Obviously she'd better answer the ad. If she had the chance of two weeks' extra salary, she could happily chaperon a dozen children.

Once her decision was made, she merely had to go back to her hotel and write the letter of application so it could be mailed that afternoon. She took a final sip of coffee, left the necessary amount of francs in the saucer on the table, and got to her feet.

Heads turned as she went by but she didn't notice. Her thoughts were already concerned with what a child's nursemaid should wear to an important job interview.

Two days later as she waited nervously in the tiny lobby of her Place Vendôme hotel, she still wasn't sure that her outfit was exactly right. Her eyes went to the clock above the reception desk. It was too late to change now. Mr. "Whoever-he-was" would arrive in five minutes.

The telephone confirmation for her application letter had come early that morning. Unfortunately she was sitting in a bakery on Rue St. Honoré at the time consuming warm French bread and *café au lait* for breakfast. The message was delivered later when she returned to the hotel.

"But what's his name?" she had asked. "This man who made the appointment. Surely he must have said."

The stocky concierge shrugged. "Sorry, mademoiselle. It was a poor connection and the gentleman spoke English rapidly. All I understood was that he will speak to you personally at ten-thirty this morning. He asked that you be prompt."

Gail's lips curled derisively. That sounded like the man in the advertisement, all right. He must be a

9

hopeless case on moral virtues. Perhaps she should wire home for money, after all. Her eyes had assessed her reflection in the wavy mirror on the wall. No! She'd be darned if she would . . . at least, not without trying for the job first.

But now, when she surveyed her appearance, the doubts came back. All in all, she wasn't the "nursemaid type." Trying for simplicity with a tailored leaf-green knit blazer over her stark white silk blouse and pleated gray skirt, she had achieved a casual sophistication instead. Even her green Italian shoes with their perky ties looked more pleasing than practical. Just minutes ago, she had brushed her hair severely but it was already beginning to cap her head in casual waves. So much for her efforts to look sedate.

"At least you can sound meek and anxious," she told her reflection. "Like an absolute paragon of virtue."

Actually if she could present a "toned-down" appearance, she should have a good chance at the job. Her references were excellent and could be confirmed by a family friend at the American embassy. He had sworn he would testify to the exemplary behavior of one Gail Alden, spinster.

She moved over to sit in an uncomfortable chair next to the black metal birdcage of an elevator and stared at the lobby door. When she thought back on it, there was only one time when that "exemplary behavior" had ever been questioned. Even now—three years later—it made her seethe to remember.

It had happened the summer after college graduation when she was working in the campus alumni office. She had accepted a dinner date with an assistant professor one night and later went back to his apartment for coffee. Unfortunately, the professor chose to swallow more brandy than coffee as the evening passed. When Gail wanted to leave, she was able to reach the hallway of his building only after a determined and noisy strug-

10

gle. She had hidden in a janitor's closet until her host had stumbled back to his apartment, slamming the door behind him. Then she had gone out into the lighted corridor and surveyed her torn blouse with disgust, wondering how on earth was she going to get home in that condition.

Without warning, the door of the elevator beside her had opened and the man emerging had almost fallen over her. He took one look at the blouse and the tears running down her cheeks before asking quietly what he could do to help.

"If you have a car, I'd appreciate a ride home," she had said, trying to keep her voice level.

"My car's in the basement." He was punching the elevator button as he spoke. "This takes us directly down there. In the meantime..." He shrugged out of his sports coat. "You'd better put this on."

Her cheeks flamed. "All I need is a safety pin."

"Sorry, I can't help you there." He had bowed her into the elevator when the door opened.

Conversation during the ride to her apartment building consisted solely of her instructions on how to get them there in the shortest possible time. After the first five minutes, Gail remembered why the lanky man at her side looked familiar; he was one of the alumni she had registered for a weekend seminar only that morning. All she could do was huddle down in the seat and hope his memory wasn't as good as hers.

Even that possibility deserted her when they drove up in front of her building. She was struggling to take off his coat when she was restrained by a firm hand on her shoulder.

"Keep it on until you get in your apartment," he instructed tersely. "You might meet someone on the way."

"But how can I get it back to you?"

"That's easy. Leave it in the Dean's office tomorrow." As her eyes widened, he continued. "Certainly I recognized you—with that hair of yours, any man would be blind not to." There was the flickering of a cynical grin. "Maybe we'd better skip any introductions . . . under the circumstances."

"I quite agree," she said stiffly.

"But if you'll accept a suggestion . . . you'd better change escorts or take along another set of clothes, after this. Next time there might not be anybody to rescue you."

"Why . . . you . . . you . . ."

"Spare me the dramatics and all that guff about a permissive society. If you hope to find a husband, this is the wrong way to go about it. Use your head, girl!" He gunned the motor impatiently. "I'll pick up my coat tomorrow."

She fled the car as if a pack of werewolves were after her and heard him drive away before she could even open the door of her building.

After a sleepless night, she decided she simply couldn't face his mocking expression the next day. She telephoned the girl who worked at the next desk and asked if she'd take the sports coat to the office. Then she called her employer and requested some time off for personal reasons. Fortunately, both requests were granted without question.

When she returned to the office the following week, the alumni seminar was stale news. There was a note of apology from the assistant professor on her desk and she consigned it to the wastebasket along with his chances for any more dates. Since the sports coat wasn't in sight, she presumed that it had gotten back to its owner. For a moment, she thought of asking and then prudently discarded the idea.

She *did* take a surreptitious look at the seminar files and discovered her rescuer's name was David Knight— an architect from Philadelphia.

12

Thank heavens, Philadelphia was miles away and she wouldn't have to worry about bumping into the objectionable man again.

Despite her determination to forget him, it took several months for his image to fade. At the strangest times his strong profile would come back to haunt her. She could still recall his piercing gray eyes and the way his tall, lanky frame folded in the driver's seat that awful night. After one of those weak moments, she had looked up his personal record in the alumni files and nodded in satisfaction. Nothing spectacular there—he'd merely turned out for the usual things when he was an undergraduate. Her glance went on down through the information. At the bottom of the card, someone had listed the honors David Knight had received in Architectural Design. Her eyes widened. For a man in his late twenties, he'd lost no time in surging to the front of his profession. She flipped the card. There was no mention of a wife in his personal biography. That wasn't surprising—with his talent for biting sarcasm, any woman in her right mind would give him a wide berth.

She replaced the card in the file and closed the drawer with a slam. So much for an unpleasant encounter! She would put him out of her mind just as she had discarded the torn blouse she had worn that night.

Gone . . . thrown away . . . pfft! Never to be seen again.

The rattle of the hotel elevator brought her back to the present. Her nose twitched as a wave of heavy perfume broke over her and she watched a plump Frenchwoman emerge and teeter across the lobby on unsuitable high heels. After her stay in Paris, Gail could testify that most of its citizens bathed regularly in wine or perfume . . . disdaining water as an unnecessary element that merely rusts and corrodes. Unfortunately,

13

the overall fragrance in the French subways at rush hours could leave a tourist reeling!

Her eyes went to the clock behind the reception desk again. Ten-thirty exactly. Now she'd see if Mr. "Highest Morals" would keep her waiting.

At that moment, the heavy glass lobby door opened under the touch of a decisive hand. Gail's glance swerved to focus on the tall, masculine figure which propelled it. The man moved automatically toward the concierge's desk before his searching look took in her hesitant, waiting form and he stopped halfway across the lobby.

"Miss Alden?" His deep voice easily bridged the intervening space.

"I'm Gail Ald . . ." Her voice trailed off in frozen horror as he approached.

Dear God—it couldn't be! Not out of two hundred million people in the United States. She was caught in that daydream of hers—but the dream had suddenly transformed to a nightmare. Take it easy, she told herself. When she looked again, the tall man in gray would be an utter stranger. Slowly she blinked and looked again.

"Miss Alden?" He pulled up, frowning. "I'm David Knight."

She sagged as if he'd used a tomahawk.

"Here! For lord's sake . . . sit down!" He half-supported, half-dragged her limp form onto a couch in the corner. "I don't understand. Are you ill?"

Desperately she tried to pull herself together . . . hoping he couldn't hear the terrified pounding of her heart. She took a deep, shuddering breath. "No—of course not. If you'll just give me a minute. . . ."

"Perhaps some coffee would help." He saw her frightened nod. "I'll ask the concierge to order it. You wait here."

"I couldn't move if I wanted to," she admitted, the words tumbling out. "Sorry, I'm not usually this way."

His smile was a polite surface effort. "I'll be right back."

She watched him stride across the lobby and her lips thinned in dismay. With luck, she had about thirty seconds to pull herself together and decide on a future course of action.

Her gaze lingered on the concierge's desk where an animated discussion was taking place. It was amazing how little the past three years had altered David Knight's appearance. Those lines of tiredness at the edge of his eyes were new . . . or perhaps his summer tan had hid them before. Now, despite the fact that it was mid-July, he looked pale and finely drawn. Otherwise he was the same—that stern jaw just as determined and his lean face set in an expression of polite forbearance.

For the moment, she felt her luck might hold. Surely if the man had recognized her, he wouldn't be trying to brace her shaky frame with a cup of coffee. Possibly she could get the job without telling him the truth.

Gail's innate sense of honesty stirred uneasily. She had never gotten a job that way in her entire life. In any event, he'd be sure to remember eventually.

"Coffee will be along practically immediately." Her prospective employer was pulling up a chair to the end of her couch and lowering himself on it. "Are you feeling better?"

"Yes, thanks." Gail hesitated and then plunged on. "Mr. Knight, I think we've met before. . . ."

"It's possible"—his bored tones cut into her sentence—"but hardly worth discussing." The solicitous look on his face had changed to cynicism.

She flushed at his unspoken implication. He must think she was trying to scrape up an acquaintance. So much for her attempts at honesty.

"The only important thing to me now is whether

15

you'll do for this job," he was saying. "That's the point of this interview."

She sat erect on the couch and tried to appear discreetly dependable. Anything to cancel her initial impression.

His forehead creased in a frown. "If you're the nervous type, I'm not sure you'll be able to cope."

"I'm *not* the nervous type," she flashed back.

He let his raised eyebrows answer while they watched a waiter wheel the coffee cart toward them.

"It's just that you startled me," Gail went on defensively. "You reminded me of someone . . . I once knew."

The waiter pulled up a round table and put the laden tray on it before withdrawing.

"I see." David gestured toward the silver coffeepot. "Will you do the honors or shall I?"

Gail thought of her still shaky fingers and clasped them in her lap. "Won't you . . . please?"

He leaned over to pour the coffee. "Want anything in it?"

"No, thanks. Just black." She accepted a steaming cup. "It smells wonderful."

"There's a plate of croissants here, too."

"Oh, I don't think . . ."

He calmly overrode her protest. "You could use some fattening up." That sharp glance of his passed over her as he transferred a roll to her plate. "Or are you on some screwball diet?"

"Not from choice," Gail said, smiling. "Have you looked at the food prices in this town? When I thought I was going to have those extra weeks here, I had to cut down on something." She nibbled on a flaky croissant. "Of course, I could wire home for money but I'd rather not. I told you about that in my application."

He nodded and helped himself to a roll.

16

She went on. "Perhaps you could tell me about the job."

"In a minute." He was concentrating on the food in front of him. "Breakfast was a little thin for me, too."

"I know what you mean. Over here, it's either four courses and takes two hours or it's a ham roll when you're standing at a counter."

At his post across the lobby, the concierge had decided they were no longer worthy of his undivided interest and he was gently snoozing, his hands folded over his ample girth. The reception desk was deserted but the sound of sporadic typing came from the office behind. Just beyond, the birdcage elevator waited for the next passenger with its grill door leaning drunkenly as a result of some missing screw.

David stared at it as he chewed. "Do people actually risk their necks in that thing?" he asked finally.

Gail nodded. "All the time. Oh, *I'm* not guilty—I take the stairs. My room's only one flight up."

"I'll be damned." He was still staring across the lobby. "The French are a funny bunch—they build the latest things like the SST and continue to use hotel elevators that should have been buried next to Marie Antoinette." He took another bite of roll. "Anyhow, stay out of that contraption."

Her lips twitched in amusement. Three years hadn't made any difference in David's manners; he was just as dictatorial as ever.

"Does that order come from a prospective employer," she asked meekly, "or is it a friendly suggestion from a fellow American?"

He looked irritated but didn't bother to answer.

She probed further. "I really want to know. I'm only human."

"The word is normal. We're all human," he pointed out coldly.

"I thought you majored in Architecture—not Basic English."

His eyes surveyed her appraisingly while he considered her comment. Then he said, "I'm also interested in having my niece hear English spoken properly."

"Your niece?" Gail put her cup down without being aware of it. "I understood the ad referred to your own child."

"Then you were wrong. Look here, Miss Alden. . . ." He leaned forward and rested his elbows on his knees. "We might as well get down to it. This job, I mean. Do you honestly want to take it on?"

"Of course—but let's go back a little. Are you satisfied with my qualifications? You *do* understand that I haven't any actual experience as a nursemaid."

He gestured impatiently. "I remember that from your application."

"But surely you must have had replies from women who were better suited to the job. . . ."

"See here, are you telling me you don't want to be hired?"

"Oh, no! I just didn't want you to think . . . " Her voice trailed off again as she realized she was making subconscious apologies for something that happened three years ago. It was obvious that David Knight hadn't connected her with that episode so she'd better forget it as well. Any more dithering on her part and he'd be out the door.

"Let's settle this once and for all," he was saying. "I'll give you the background for the job and then you can make your decision. Is it a deal?"

Gail smiled in relief. "Unless it involves white slavery or walking on red-hot coals, you've hired yourself a nursemaid."

He looked much younger as he grinned in response. "Then you're on. If you'll pour us another cup of
18

coffee, I'll rattle the family skeletons. You may decide that you prefer a white slaver, after all."

"I doubt that. Try me."

He offered cigarettes, lit them, and settled back. "Okay, but I wasn't kidding about the skeletons."

"Don't worry," she assured him, "I have a few relatives stashed in the closet, too."

"Who'd have thought we were kindred souls?" he murmured. "Actually, my story starts with my father's wives. Hey . . . don't look like that! There were only two of them." His grin widened as she relaxed. "Dad was originally married to a wealthy Spanish woman who died quite young and left her estate to their daughter Margarita. A few years later, my mother came along . . . married Dad . . . and I appeared in due course. All of us felt sorry for Margarita when she was growing up so we spoiled her rotten. When she got married some time ago to a man she met in Madrid, she wasn't happy about settling down the way Ricardo thought she should."

"Ricardo's her husband?"

He nodded. "Ricardo Gomez. He's a nice fellow except that he has pretty stiff-necked Spanish ideas about a wife's role in the scheme of things. Margarita was a textile designer before they were married and she wouldn't retire to lounge around the house all day in approved European fashion. They spent most of the first year fighting. Fortunately, there was a lull in hostilities when Pippa arrived—she's my niece who's eight years old now. Everything was going along fine until seven months ago."

"What happened then?"

"Margarita claimed Ricardo was dazzled by some acquaintance of theirs. They had a real blowup and Margarita left for London . . . taking Pippa with her, of course. Her lawyers arranged a separation agreement which gave Pippa's father visitation rights every six months. So . . . for the past three weeks—Ricardo's had Pippa with him in Spain. Margarita asked me to bring her back to London since I was to be in the neighborhood. That was fine with me. Originally I'd planned to retrieve Pippa the day I went back to England but, like you, I had to change my plans. Now I need another ten days or so in Portugal and Spain. Margarita won't hear of any date change on the visitation clause so I have to get my niece the day I promised." David leaned forward to grind out his cigarette in a china ash tray. "Actually Pippa's a good little kid and nice to have around but an uncle can't manage in hotels with an eight-year-old niece who's practically a stranger." He sounded sheepish. "I don't know which of us would be more petrified."

"From what I know of eight-year-old girls—I imagine you would," Gail said, putting out her own cigarette. "Is Pippa a nickname?"

"That's right. Short for Felipa. She's a shy little thing. Her Spanish upbringing has made her less forthcoming than most American youngsters her age."

"She must have taken her parents' separation pretty hard."

David's lips compressed into a straight line of dissatisfaction. "Damnably hard. I'd like to knock Margarita's and Ricardo's heads together. We're all hoping they work things out eventually."

Gail nodded sympathetically. "I'll be glad to help, of course, if you feel Pippa should have a woman along. It's a pity your wife isn't with you." Her last comment was essayed tentatively and she watched for his reaction.

It wasn't long coming. "That would be difficult"—his tone was dry—"since I'm not married. I thought I'd made that clear, Miss Alden."

"No—I didn't know." Inexplicably her heart was thudding faster than usual. "I hope I can fill the bill."

20

She went on hastily, "As a nursemaid for Pippa, of course."

"I didn't think you were applying for the other position."

Realizing she was beaten in that exchange, she sought another subject. "When did you want to pick up Pippa?"

"Tomorrow. I have reservations on the Lisbon Express leaving Gare D'Austerlitz at three o'clock this afternoon."

"This afternoon! You *do* believe in moving quickly."

"I told you I had to keep on schedule. There'll be a car and driver waiting for us in Lisbon tomorrow noon. We can start north for Obidos right away."

"Obidos?" She felt like a parrot, mimicking his words.

Evidently he was thinking the same thing. "Obidos," he repeated with some irritation. "That's where Pippa has been staying for the past week."

"Why Portugal? I thought her father was Spanish."

"He is. She's been visiting her old Portuguese nursemaid who now lives in Obidos." He smiled slowly as he watched her face lighten with comprehension. "All clear now? I believe you were worried about white slavery after all."

In her confusion, she blushed. "Don't be absurd, Mr. Knight. I'm quite able to take care of myself."

"So I see. . . ."

The color in her cheeks deepened. "I've explained why I need this job. Emergencies can happen to anybody . . . even you."

"*Touché.*" He touched his forehead in mock salute. "Maybe we'd better admit we need each other badly for the next two weeks. After that, we can go our independent ways. Agreed, Miss Alden?"

"Agreed, Mr. Knight." Her hand was suddenly engulfed in his but the next thing she knew he had dropped it hastily as if embarrassed by his spontaneous gesture.

He stood up abruptly. "If you haven't any more questions, I'll come by for you in a cab at two-fifteen. Don't be late—the traffic getting to the Left Bank is terrible and I don't want to miss the train."

"I'll be ready."

He made an uncertain move toward his wallet. "Perhaps you'd like an advance on your salary. . . ."

"No, thank you." Her reply was stiff. "It isn't at all necessary."

His acknowledging nod was equally formal. "Whatever you say, Miss Alden. I'll see you at two-fifteen."

That afternoon, his taxi stopped in front of the hotel precisely as the ormolu clock on the reception desk was chiming the quarter hour.

Gail stood waiting near the entrance with her two bags at her feet. By the time the cab driver had opened the door for her and unlocked his trunk for the luggage, the hall porter was on hand to transfer the suitcases.

He accepted her tip with a jerky bow. *"Merci, mille fois. Au revoir, Mademoiselle Alden . . . Monsieur."* His nod took in David, who was standing by the open taxi door.

"Watch your head," her employer counseled as she started to get in the car.

His words startled her so that she collapsed onto the back seat rather than achieving the dignified entry she had planned. Flustered, she retrieved her handbag from the floor and withdrew to the far corner.

David got in and slammed the door. "Gare D'Austerlitz," he instructed the driver, who nodded and started off with a jerk that threw them against the back of the seat. "We won't have to worry about being late," David went on. "This fellow's on one of the trial runs for the Indianapolis Five Hundred." There was a screech of brakes as they turned the corner into Rue de Rivoli.

"I see what you mean," Gail murmured, clinging to the door handle.

The cab sped past the colorful Jardin des Tuileries fronting the Louvre.

David nodded toward the famous museum. "Did you enjoy the *Mona Lisa* and all the rest?"

"Very much," she assured him, "once I found out where to go. There was a grouchy guard on duty who was determined not to give visitors any directions."

"Maybe he'd had a bad day," David said tactfully.

"Mmmm." She wasn't convinced.

"Other than that . . . did you like Paris?"

"Oh, yes . . . but I couldn't get used to wine being cheaper than milk."

"Only the tourists drink milk."

"I found that out." She smiled crookedly. "Isn't it strange how silly things make an impression on a person?"

"What do you mean?"

"Well, I still stare when I see these people carry around those long loaves of French bread. They wield them the way an Englishman does an umbrella." As the car whipped around a corner, she found herself flung against his gray suit jacket. "I'm sorry." She pulled back, embarrassed. "If our speed demon can't qualify for the Indy, he should try the Grand Prix de Monaco."

"My God, don't suggest it."

"I won't." She yanked her skirt back down to her knees. "How was your stay in Paris?"

"Par for the course, I guess. From an architect's viewpoint, the city's magnificent. That makes up for some of the irritating little things like having to rent a bench every time you want to sit down in a park."

"I hope you managed to get 'round that other European custom of sharing train sleeping compartments with strangers."

"There shouldn't be any trouble. I was able to get a compartment with two berths and bought both of them." There was no reply and he glanced up to find her frowning.

"Both berths?" she asked carefully.

"That's right," he began before comprehension dawned. "Sorry, I meant to say that I got two compartments for us. Two separate compartments . . . with two berths in each. . . ." He broke off his labored explanation as she started to laugh.

"Making four berths in all," she couldn't resist saying.

He grinned in response. "Two for you and two for me. If you're wise, you'll pile your suitcases on the top one. Even though it's bought and paid for—some European train conductors have larceny in their hearts and can't stand to see a berth unoccupied. It happened to me going through Germany once. They sold the top berth a second time and I ended up with an old duck who slept with his cap on and snored loudly enough to be heard in the next country."

"What did you do?"

"Sat up most of the night in the deserted diner. At least, I was first in line for breakfast." He peered out the cab window. "There's the station ahead of us. We'll have time to spare."

Gail ran her fingers through her hair and smoothed her blazer collar as the driver turned in the entrance. "Do we buy sandwiches on the platform for our dinner tonight?"

"No—there's a dining car on the train. I'll try to get the first sitting for us. We don't even have to change trains at the Spanish border. That's one reason I was anxious to catch the express."

She looked confused.

"They have different gauge tracks in Spain and Portugal," he explained. "On the express trains they merely change wheels on the cars at the border station; on the locals, the passengers have to transfer into a completely different train. Usually in the middle of the night," he added reminiscently as their taxi pulled up to the curb. "Right now you can make yourself useful and hail a porter while I pay the driver."

"All right, Mr. Knight." She hesitated before asking, "Will you take care of my bags or shall I . . . ?"

"Naturally I'll take care of them." He opened the door. "Your duties don't start until Obidos, Miss Alden." He broke off as their driver erupted from behind the steering wheel. The man was gesturing wildly and spouting a torrent of French. "What the devil is the matter with him?" David asked.

Gail had to raise her voice. "He's explaining about the extra charge for baggage and wants to know the number of our train."

"Here!" David shoved a handful of francs into her hand. "You take care of the luggage and pay him. I'll snag a porter. And you can take that smug look off your face, Miss Alden, or I'll get my revenge later on."

She was enjoying the drama. "Exactly what kind of revenge did you have in mind?"

He looked amused. "It's going to be hard to explain to the conductor why one couple needs two compartments and four berths. My French may not be up to it."

"I wasn't hired to translate," she pointed out, "I'm merely the nursemaid."

"Then you may find yourself a nursemaid with a roommate."

"Oh, surely not." Her eyes sparkled with laughter. "Is that a threat or a promise?"

"Well, I don't wear a nightcap and I don't snore. . . ."

25

She decided they'd fenced long enough. "I appreciate your confidences," she said, matching his solemn tone, "but I don't think you have to worry."

"No?"

"No. Any trouble like that and *I'll* sit in the diner to be first in line for breakfast." Instead of angering him with that ultimatum, she saw a satisfied expression spread over his face.

He stared thoughtfully at her a moment longer and then strode across the station platform to hail a porter.

Gail turned to count out francs in their driver's hand . . . while wondering exactly what the next two weeks would bring.

CHAPTER TWO

Gail was still blessing the fates that made her read the "Help Wanted" column in Paris as she sat happily in her compartment the next forenoon and watched the colorful Portuguese countryside flash by. Although the train was only forty minutes from Lisbon, they were still traveling through rich farmland that was cultivated to the very last inch.

All morning they had passed through miles of silvery olive trees which seemed to grow with equal ease on the steep hillsides or the rocky soil of the valleys. Then came the patchwork fields of corn—some of the green cornstalks were shorter than their midwestern counterparts but they looked sturdy and healthy nonetheless.

Every few minutes, Gail would see men and women working in the fields; the wives dressed in black or somber gray and their husbands in sweat-stained undershirts and baggy cotton pants. They would look up to smile and wave good-naturedly as the train passed but before it was out of sight, they were once again bent over endless rows of vegetables and fruit.

Most of the Portuguese villages were on hillsides and looked much like their Italian replicas with red-tiled roofs, immaculate whitewashed houses, and pots of geraniums on the windowsills to provide vivid splashes of color. In the smaller towns where there weren't automatic railroad signal gates, tiny old women who were always black-shawled and silver-haired would stand at the rail crossing with their red warning flags to keep the traffic safely away. Not that there was much traffic for them to protect . . . for other than an occasional wagon drawn by a yoke of oxen or a worn cart pulled by a well-fed donkey, the winding roads were bare.

It was like stepping back into a book from the past, Gail decided, and she wished there was time to linger for a chapter or two before arriving at bustling, modern Lisbon.

She heaved a blissful sigh and let her head rest against the velour seat. Everything had been so peaceful since Paris that she wondered now why she had ever worried. The train compartments had been properly reserved, clean, and fortunately empty. When the sleeping car porter was informed of the single occupancy for each one, he had merely given a deep Gallic shrug which meant "if Americans choose to waste their money why should he care"! Then his pitying glance lingered on Gail and made her realize he thought she was a forsaken woman. She had lifted her chin a little higher at that and proceeded to ignore him until time to surrender her passport.

"I will return it, madame . . . er . . . mademoiselle, before we arrive at Lisbon," he said, scooping it up. "In the meantime, you must complete these. . . ." He thrust two customs declarations into her hands. "I will collect them later when I make up the berths."

"The berth," she corrected. Then, at his puzzled stare: "You make up only one berth . . . remember?"

"*Certainement*, if that is what mademoiselle wishes. Oh yes! Monsieur Knight desired that I should give you this." He presented a dinner ticket for the early sitting as if he were conferring the Legion of Merit.

"Thank you," Gail said, wondering why David

couldn't have brought it himself. Was she supposed to go to dinner alone?

The porter dusted some chrome trim with his cuff. "He also said that he will stop by when they ring the . . ." He murmured, *"Comment dit-on gong en anglais?"*

"You say 'gong'—the same as in French," she told him absently.

"Merci, mademoiselle," he said, bestowing a sour look on her. If the woman could speak French, why was he bothering with English? *"A bientôt."*

"Oui," she replied politely and watched him shut the compartment door.

Dinner marked David's first appearance since they had boarded the train. He had changed into a comfortable cotton sports coat and slacks but his face was drawn with pain.

"Is something wrong?" she had asked as she opened the compartment door at his knock.

"Why should anything be wrong?" He pushed a pair of dark glasses higher on the bridge of his nose. "Didn't you hear the gong for dinner?"

"Of course . . . I'm ready." She turned to get her purse from the seat. "I meant you. You look . . ." She started to say "ghastly" and then searched for a better word.

"Lousy," he supplied.

"How about . . . tired? Don't you feel well?"

"It's just a headache. I get migraines sometimes."

"Then you won't want to go in to dinner."

"Of course I do. We have to eat." He winced as a sharp curve in the track threw them against the side of the sleeping car. "Come on . . . we'd better move. French cooks don't wait for anyone."

Despite his assertion that he felt fine, Gail noticed that he barely touched the elaborate dinner served to them. For a moment, she wished they were on an

American train where one could order something simple rather than having to struggle through cold salmon appetizers, vegetable omelet, and then a hefty slice of roast veal. The dining car was old-fashioned and crowded with people but the service by French waiters was impeccable.

They had been seated at a table for four and their companions were two Frenchmen in their late twenties casually dressed in the body shirts and skin-tight slacks that were so popular in Paris. Both men spoke excellent English which they had learned during a year spent in a Detroit advertising agency while they serviced automobile accounts. At the moment, they were on a holiday from their Paris office and were en route to a southern Portuguese beach resort.

Dinner conversation flowed easily across the table although Gail noticed that David did more listening than anything else. He sat with his eyes narrowed as if the glare from a spectacular sunset they were viewing bothered him. Occasionally he took off his dark glasses and rubbed his forehead wearily.

When coffee was finally served, the two Frenchmen invited Gail to join them in the lounge car for an after-dinner drink. She refused politely and followed David back down the aisle to their car. He remained silent all the while but she couldn't decide whether it was from his headache or her friendliness with the young Frenchmen.

"You weren't much help on that invitation," she said finally as they reached the end of their sleeping car.

He didn't pretend to misunderstand. "I didn't intend to be. You're of legal age, Miss Alden—if you want to spend the evening in the lounge car with a couple of Romeos . . . feel free to do it."

Gail stared at him in bewilderment. The way she had behaved at dinner had done nothing to warrant this coldness.

30

"I didn't want to spend the evening in the lounge car." Her voice was just as firm as his. "I work for you, Mr. Knight, and you obviously don't feel well. Perhaps there's something I can do . . ."

"My God, I told you that your job doesn't start until we get Pippa." He paused by his compartment door, his face drawn with pain. "How many times do I have to repeat it! Until then, I can certainly take care of myself. Good night, Miss Alden!" Halfway through the door he stopped and looked over his shoulder. "And I *don't* need anybody to tuck me in." The door was closed securely behind him.

Gail wished she could haul off and give that . . . door . . . a good swift kick. So much for her attempt to pacify her employer. For a minute, she almost wished she'd accepted the invitation of the Frenchmen. Then she shrugged, murmured a few words about bears with sore heads, and continued down the corridor to her compartment.

David's admonition didn't daunt her completely, however. In feminine fashion, she tried again later that evening.

"Georges," she confronted the porter when he was making up her berth, "Monsieur Knight . . . in compartment G . . . is not feeling well. Would you be kind enough to see if there's anything he needs?"

Whether it was because of her careful French phrasing or the anxious look on her pretty face, Georges nonetheless hastened to reassure her. "Monsieur is feeling better. He has taken medicine for the migraine and is now sleeping. I shall check again later."

Evidently he did, for at breakfast time he told Gail that "Monsieur" was much improved. "He requests that you breakfast without him, however." He laid a flat palm on his brass-buttoned uniform chest. "I, myself, took croissants and tea to Monsieur Knight an hour ago."

Gail smiled at the memory of that virtuous proclamation. Then she looked at her watch and her smile faded. Only twenty minutes now before their Lisbon arrival and Georges would undoubtedly want to carry her bags to the end of the car well before they reached the city limits. She'd better get ready.

David's tall form didn't appear in the doorway of her compartment until the train was actually in the Lisbon station and slowing to a stop.

"Good morning . . . or is it afternoon?" he said tersely. "I hope you're ready to go."

Gail's tone was equally formal. "All ready, thanks, and I think it's afternoon." Her quick glance showed that he seemed back to normal but apparently was still feeling the aftereffects of the headache. He was wearing dark glasses and holding his head and shoulders stiffly.

The train jolted to a stop and the strident shouts of porters and platform vendors merged to blast the calm of their car.

"Come on." David urged her out into the corridor. "I've told Georges to give our bags to a porter. He's to bring them out to the taxi rank . . . that's where our car and driver will be waiting."

They were.

A man wearing a black chauffeur's jacket was standing by the door of a highly polished Mercedes-Benz, watching the passengers pour out onto the depot platform.

"That should be it," David said, striding ahead of Gail. "I'll find out."

Gail smiled as she obediently hovered a few feet away. David still wasn't wasting any time with unnecessary pleasantries. For all the interest he exhibited, she might as well have been the passing pushcart vendor selling box lunches, bottles of wine, and bags of paper-wrapped candies.

32

She glanced away from his display to find David beckoning peremptorily.

"Miss Alden!"

"Yes, Mr. Knight." As she moved obediently forward, she wished for a second that she'd contributed to the Women's Lib cause before she'd left home. This man made her feel like a coolie.

"Miss Alden . . . this is Josef Taliaferro who will be driving us."

She tried to remember the proper Portuguese greeting . . . only to find it was completely unnecessary.

"Good afternoon, Miss Alden. I hope you had a pleasant trip." Josef's jerky bow suited his short, wiry build. He was about forty and soberly dressed in a white shirt and gray whipcord pants under the black jacket. His curly hair was very dark and the darkness was repeated in a pair of alert eyes set deeply below a narrow forehead. Like many Portuguese men, the bone structure of his face was particularly good with prominent cheekbones that were a throwback to ancient Greek profiles.

He gestured toward the shadowed interior of the car. "If you'd like to step in—I'll take care of your bags. It's unfortunate that you've arrived in our midday heat. During the summer, Lisbon gets very hot."

She murmured an automatic agreement but looked up at David before moving. "Shall I sit in front?" she asked him.

It would be nice to know whether he expected her to sit beside Josef as befitted her nursemaid status.

"Don't be a damned fool!" David told her flatly as Josef walked down the curb to hail their porter. "Get in the back and stop cringing, for God's sake. You make me feel like Uriah Heep."

"I'm not surprised . . . after the way you talked last night."

"Then I'd better apologize, hadn't I," he said coolly. "*Now* will you get in."

Only partially appeased, she did as he asked. Then she deliberately looked out the car window as David sandwiched his long form onto the seat beside her.

Crowded tram cars were clanging down the busy street, ignoring the throngs of people who deserted the busy sidewalks to jaywalk in front of them. A sturdy policeman in a gray khaki uniform stood on a raised traffic box at the intersection and his long white gauntlets flashed as he gestured to keep order in the bumper-to-bumper automobiles. Occasionally his whistle would shrill in protest as a driver ignored his directions. Then came the squeal of brakes and shouts of derision until the hapless offender extricated himself from the traffic chaos.

The stone buildings of the Alfama or Old Lisbon rose on the hill directly behind the boulevard. To the right of the Lisbon rail terminal, the broad river Tagus flowed . . . the wide marine thoroughfare nearly as crowded with freighters and smaller fishing craft as the street was with surface traffic.

Gail could see the huge superstructure of the largest drydock in the world and, by craning her head, could view Lisbon's answer to San Francisco's Golden Gate bridge. This was called the Ponte Salazar and looked like a curving concrete arrow across the Tagus to the tremendous statue of Christ on the opposite hill. For a second, she thought nostalgically of the quiet Portuguese countryside and then she decided the excitement of modern Lisbon affected her just as strongly.

"Enjoying the view?" David asked softly.

"It's tremendous!" Her irritation was forgotten. "Will we stay long in the city?"

"Not this time," he said cryptically as he watched Josef get behind the steering wheel. "Have you got the directions straight, Josef?"

"Certainly, Senhor Knight. We go to Obidos as you said. First though, I must drive to my garage and tell the man in charge that your plans have changed. Perhaps you and Miss Alden want lunch in the interval?"

David started to demur and then reconsidered as he noted Gail's excited face. "All right, I suppose that's a good idea. Take us uptown by the park. We'll decide where to lunch on the way."

"What park are you talking about?" Gail asked.

David sat back in his corner of the seat. "They have a big one here named after Eduardo the Seventh. This street leads up to it. The city plan was redesigned by the Marquis de Pombal after the big earthquake in seventeen fifty-five. The city fathers even named a style of architecture after him in gratitude."

"Then this is a busman's holiday for you."

"Sort of. At least it's one of the reasons why I wanted the extra days in Spain and Portugal. There are some ideas over here that should fit nicely into a project my firm has been commissioned to do." His glance became speculative. "You look as if you'd been given an extra Christmas suddenly."

"That's the way I feel . . . I'm so thrilled to be here. My vacation budget didn't stretch even to the borders of Spain and Portugal. This is all one tremendous bonus." She gestured expansively.

He pushed his sunglasses farther up his nose. "Then maybe there's hope, after all."

She abandoned her vigil through the car window to turn and stare at him. "What do you mean by that?"

"I'll tell you in a minute. There's the park of Eduardo the Seventh right ahead of us." He leaned forward. "Josef . . . let us off at the Hotel Dom Joao on the next block. The food's supposed to be good there."

"Very good food," Josef confirmed. "I shall come back and park in front in exactly two hours . . . if that is all right."

35

"Good enough. No . . . don't bother to get out," David told him as the car stopped. He opened the rear door and helped Gail onto the sidewalk. Beside her, he closed the door and nodded a casual dismissal to Josef. "We'll see you later."

Gail watched the car reenter the traffic on the wide thoroughfare and then followed David up some marble steps to the entrance of a busy modern hotel.

"Ready for lunch?" he asked as they entered the lobby.

"Yes, thanks . . . if I'm dressed well enough for this place." She apprehensively surveyed the entrance of the glass-doored dining room where a maître d'hôtel hovered and then looked dubiously down at the pleated skirt of her white knit which she was wearing with a dark brown blouse. A matching white sweater was thrown casually over her shoulders. "I think I'm missing a few things . . . like a sable coat or a waist-length string of pearls."

"Don't be an idiot," David replied with gratifying promptness and steered her toward the headwaiter.

When they were seated at a window table overlooking the garden, he glanced across an expanse of damask to find her reading the elaborate menu.

He grinned at her look of horror. "Want me to order?" he asked.

"If you don't . . . it's going to be sign language all the way." She indicated a printed heading. "What does this say?"

He stared at where she pointed. "Dinner."

"That's what I mean." She closed the menu resignedly. "I'm in your hands."

David nodded. "Never mind. You're still ahead on points after that bout with our French taxi driver." He was perusing the menu. "The fish is good in Portugal. All right with you?" He glanced up for her approval and then signaled to the dining room captain. When they were alone again, he asked, "Now, what were we talking about?"

She leaned toward him, liking the way his eyes had softened on that last question. "What did you mean about there being hope . . . just before we got out of the car?"

"I was still apologizing for the way I acted last night," he confessed grimly, "and I wasn't anxious to share everything with Josef."

"Oh, that! Forget it."

"I'd like to," he admitted. "Anyhow, thanks for having the porter check on me after all the hubbub."

"He wasn't supposed to tell you," she said wryly.

"I gathered that." He fingered the stem of his water goblet. "There was no need for me to act like a pompous jerk because of a simple headache."

"Migraines aren't 'simple' headaches. You're not completely over it yet, are you?"

"You see too much," he told her. Nervously he raked a hand through his dark hair. "Lunch will help."

"Probably," she agreed. "Have you been working too hard?"

He shrugged it off. "Actually, I lost out to a flu bug just before I got over here. But the fact remains, I hired a nurse for Pippa. . . ."

". . . Not for you. I remember." She leaned on her forearms as she sat forward on her chair. "It's just that this job is new to me and I could do with some practice before I meet your niece. So . . . if you wouldn't mind too much. . . ."

His laugh rang out. "All right, I give up. What do you suggest, Nurse Alden?"

"How about a nice cup of tea to start things off . . . and I hope you ordered something easy to digest like a clear soup."

"Beef consomme," he concurred. "I thought you might like one of their regional specialties." He leaned

37

back as their waiter approached. "Shout out if you don't like it."

Gail stared at the huge soup dish which was put in front of her. Chunks of bread and boiled potatoes were floating in a steaming broth which was liberally laced with garlic. At least three hard-boiled egg yolks bobbed on the surface next to chopped green onion tops.

"This is the soup course?" she asked faintly.

"Just the soup," her employer affirmed. "Fish, salad, and dessert still to come."

She got another whiff of the garlic and reeled backward. "If I ate that, I couldn't ride in the same car with you. You'd have to put me in the trunk for the rest of the trip."

David's shoulders shook with laughter as he beckoned the waiter. "Another order of consomme, please."

Gail watched the swift exchange of dishes. "He speaks English?"

"Certainly. This is a tourist hotel . . . they can't let the Americans and British starve to death. I was just showing off my Portuguese vocabulary," he admitted, watching her spoon hungrily into a cup of consomme. "Since we're going to be together for a while, do you think we could drop some of this formality?"

She met his gaze frankly. "Josef would probably expect you to call me Gail . . . but I'm not sure it's proper for me."

"Now look . . . every time you say 'Mr. Knight' I look around for my cane. And to hell with Josef," he added inconsequentially.

"All right . . . David." Her eyes gleamed with mischief. "I'll try to say it with the right amount of awe. By the way, what did you do to Josef that he was so upset?"

"You mean in the car? Damned if I know. All I did was say my plans had changed and that we weren't going directly to Seville as I'd originally thought."

38

"It's strange that it bothered him so much. Can't they give you another driver if Josef doesn't want to follow the new schedule?"

"He wouldn't hear of it." David shook his head. "I can't understand his reasoning. He was almost as upset by that idea as my change in plans. Maybe he works on a commission or something and needs the money."

"Or maybe he had a date tonight with a lady in Seville."

"Too bad . . . she'll look just as good a couple of days from now." David paused as the waiter removed their soup cups and served crisply fried fish. "You should enjoy that hake. Seafood is generally terrific in this country."

Gail took a tentative taste and smiled agreement. "Delicious! I hope I don't gain ten pounds while I'm here."

David appraised her figure casually. "You can stand a little extra weight. Not that what you have isn't very well distributed."

"Thank you very much."

He grinned. "All right, I'll change the subject. It's too bad we don't have more time to spend in Lisbon so you could do some sightseeing. After we collect Pippa, we'll come back and linger a while."

"I'd like that. Tonight we'll be at Obidos?"

He nodded and signaled the waiter for his coffee. "We'll stay at the *estalagem* there."

"The what?"

"*Estalagem* . . . Portuguese for inn. Less plush than a hotel but bigger than a *pensao*."

"I see." She rested her fork on the edge of her plate and used a slice of lemon. "I'm sorry to be so ignorant about all this but there wasn't time to get a book on Portugal before I left Paris."

"Meaning that you would have normally?"

"Of course." Her eyebrows rose in surprise. "I like to

39

know the history of a country. Why is that surprising?"

"You don't look the type for historical research."

"Well, I am," she snapped, familiar with the turn the conversation was taking. She should be; she'd heard it often enough over the years. "Surely you realize that women can't be categorized into 'types.' "

"Oh, I don't know. . . ."

"I do!"

"There's no need to take my head off." His quiet words made her guiltily aware of her raised voice. "Remember," he added jokingly, "it's still in a weakened condition from last night."

Obviously she should have remembered. Not only that, there was no reason to be so sensitive about a silly subject.

Gail stared at her plate and tried to frame an appropriate apology. She couldn't very well say, "I'm sorry, David—I didn't want you to get the wrong idea again. Not after that night three years ago." She stole a look at him from under lowered lashes.

He sat calmly drinking his coffee. If he were harboring any dark thoughts, they certainly weren't apparent.

"You should never lose your temper at mealtime," he finally murmured to her as the waiter placed a basket of fresh fruit on the table. "Haven't you heard that old oriental proverb:

> If you want your dinner
> Don't insult the cook.

I might make you run behind the car all the way to Obidos just to get even."

Gail felt about as old as Pippa after that amused reproval. "I'm sorry, Mr. Knight."

"So you should be. I expected temperament from a Portuguese driver like Josef but not from a sensible young lady from Ohio." He noted the way her lips

40

tightened at his prosaic description and his grin broadened. "Do you object to being called 'sensible,' as well, Miss Alden?"

Gail felt a flush go across her cheeks. "You have me so confused by now that I don't know what type I am. Could we please start over?"

He laughed outright at her plaintive words. "I think we'd better . . . for the sake of our digestion if nothing else. Will you have some dessert?"

"No, thank you." She sat back in her chair, relieved that he'd dropped the subject. After they'd just achieved a friendly relationship, she was loath to scuttle it. Besides, she much preferred his amiable side. She frowned slightly at that description. Amiable wasn't a strong enough word. No, when David set his mind to being agreeable, he was almost impossible to resist. And she had the sneaking suspicion that he knew it!

Josef too, was displaying urbane charm when they got back in the car at the appointed time.

"Everything all right now?" David asked him as the Mercedes slid smoothly out into the traffic.

"Everything is fine, Senhor Knight. I have told them at my garage and then I went home and had my wife put two more clean shirts in my suitcase."

So I was wrong about the girl in Seville, Gail decided. She turned to meet David's quizzical expression. Evidently he remembered their conversation too.

"How long before we reach Obidos, Josef?" she asked hurriedly.

"We should arrive about dinner time, Miss Alden. That's if we drive the scenic route along the coast."

Gail looked at David. "Are we being scenic?"

"We might as well, I suppose. All right, Josef. You choose the way and tell us what we should hear as we go along."

That leisurely drive through northern Portugal provided one of the pleasantest afternoons Gail had ever spent.

Their car followed narrow roads that sometimes cut through the steep hillsides but generally wound leisurely around them. There were the usual village clusters of whitewashed buildings and deserted streets. Generally the only occupants in evidence were thin dogs sleeping in the shade or fat donkeys standing patiently by the roadside.

"Where do all the people go?" Gail asked once after they had sped down a deserted main street. "Honestly, these places are like ghost towns—the houses always have the shutters pulled tight and the doors are locked. I don't understand it at all."

"These are farming villages, Miss Alden," Josef said over his shoulder. "The men and their wives are out in the fields during the day. Only the old people and the babies are left at home. It's the custom to keep the windows closed and shaded."

"I suppose it's cooler that way," she admitted, "but it's so desolate."

"It only looks that way from the street. Our village people lead contented lives."

"Ummm. I'll take your word for it." Her attention was caught by a grove of trees at the roadside. "Oh, look! They're peeling cork."

"It only happens every nine years," David told her. He leaned forward. "Josef, pull off to the side and we'll take a closer look."

"I don't want to make us late," Gail protested.

"Don't be silly," David replied as Josef stopped on the shoulder of the road. "This won't take a minute and the next time you see a cork in a bottle—you'll appreciate it."

Josef was already beckoning them over to a sturdy tree whose two-inch thick bark was being pulled away in a big slab. He told Gail, "If they do this oftener than

42

the nine-year interval—the tree would die. They start harvesting the trees when they're twenty to twenty-five years old."

"How long do they continue?" she asked.

"Until the tree is between one hundred twenty and one hundred fifty years old. There is one giant still standing that is more than a thousand years old."

She touched the rich brown underbark of the trunk respectfully. "Imagine a crop lasting more than a lifetime!"

"Cork has made much money for Portugal in the past." Josef was fingering a splintered piece. "Now the market has gone to plastics so the forests are losing their importance."

"Like the rubber trees in Malaysia," David put in. "They're uprooting acres of them because of synthetic rubber."

"What do they grow instead?" Josef asked.

"Palm nuts mostly . . . there's a big market for the oil. I suppose your farmers will find a substitute crop as well."

Josef shrugged. "If God wishes." He tossed the jagged piece back on the ground and brushed his hands. "Now—shall we stop at Peniche for some refreshment? It's a fishing village up the road where the children are renowned for their lace-making."

David pretended to grumble as he handed Gail back in the car. "No hanging around the place for longer than it takes you to buy a lemonade and one lace-trimmed handkerchief."

Josef heard him. "Wait and see, senhor. You'll want to meet the children too. Some of their lace-makers are barely five years old." He started the car and pulled out onto the road while he was explaining. "Years ago, the ladies of Peniche were the lace-makers but they could not earn much money that way. So, when the fish canneries were built, all the wives and mothers went to

43

work there instead. But they hated to have their heritage die so they established a lace-making school to teach their children the art. The young ones will charm you with their pins and bobbins. You'll see, Senhor Knight."

"And Senhor Knight did," Gail teased David later that afternoon as they left the lace-making school and were walking to the car. "How many handkerchiefs did you buy, for heaven's sake?"

Embarrassed, David looked down at the package he was clutching. "I don't know. Who counts? They were ridiculously cheap."

"Weren't they! And such beautiful workmanship." She glanced at her own package and said happily, "We must have bought everything they had to sell."

David managed to shove his parcel into his jacket pocket. "Oh, well—handkerchiefs won't be hard to get rid of. I expect Pippa would like another present."

"I'm sure she would . . . or any other female."

David refused to be drawn. "Uh-huh," he muttered noncommittally and caught at her elbow as they reached an intersection. "Hold on, we'd better let that procession get by."

Gail stared down the block at the throng of people headed by a village priest who were marching up the center of the dirt street.

"What is it?" she asked as plaintive sounds of weeping reached her ears.

"I'd guess a funeral. Yes . . . there's the casket being carried in the middle of the crowd."

"I see it," she said uneasily, unused to such naked grief as on the lined faces of the people shuffling past them.

David felt a shudder pass through her body and glanced down inquiringly. "What's wrong?"

"Nothing really." She attempted a smile. "Funerals

are depressing . . . even if you're not personally involved."

"You need some food to revive you." He urged her across the dusty road. "We'll have to hurry if we get our afternoon eating over in time to have dinner on schedule in Obidos."

Gail made a valiant effort to shake off her depression. "If I keep on eating according to your plan, I'll gain twenty pounds instead of ten. It'll take me the rest of the year to lose it."

"Then you'll have something to do during the long winter months," he said without a trace of remorse. "C'mon, I'm hungry."

Dusk was just starting to fall when they finally reached the old walled city of Obidos. With its fortresslike stone battlement edging the crest of the hillside, the ancient town looked like an art masterpiece from another century.

When Gail said so in awestruck tones, David promptly agreed with her.

"And you can take your choice about which one," he said. "The walls were rebuilt in the twelfth, fourteenth, and sixteenth centuries. That's after the Moors put them up originally. You can still see the castle at the very top. The government's turned it into a *pousada* these days."

"That's a rest house?"

He nodded. "We'll try to inspect it tomorrow morning. There's just about time now to collect Pippa and check in at our hotel."

Gail was staring down the cobblestone street. "Why do they need a traffic light at the archway in the wall? There isn't any intersection."

"The streets are so narrow they have to have it. A car can barely squeeze through—let alone pass anything. See what I mean?" he said as Josef eased the Mercedes gently under the rampart and into the town itself. "Do you still have that address for the nurse?" David asked him.

Josef waved a piece of paper reassuringly. "Right here, senhor. The house should be up this street near the castle."

Gail was so busy looking out the car window that she scarcely heard their conversation. The car was traveling through a solid front of whitewashed buildings looming so close on either side of the car that she could have reached out and touched them. Sprays of bougainvillea and oleander bushes decorated the walls and made a riot of color in front of grilled windows and wrought iron balconies. Displays of Portuguese pottery and raffia animals were piled high in the open doorways but the smiling shopkeepers were generally engaged in animated discussions with their neighbors, leaving the tourists to browse at will.

"Look at those tiles on that rack," Gail said rapturously. "They're gorgeous!"

"*And* heavy." David was firm. "You'll see them every place so there's no point in carrying them any farther than you have to. I'll have to clamp down on you or we won't be able to get in the car."

She looked rueful and sighed. "Guilty, your honor. Heaven knows how I'll get all my stuff home as it is. You'd better be firm."

"Remember that when I drag you out of the shops from now on. . . . Maybe you should wait in the car while I retrieve Pippa," he added teasingly. "If I remember correctly, Margarita said that the nurse's family ran an antique shop."

"Quite right, senhor." Josef was listening to their conversation. "There's the shop ahead—where the sign says *Antiguadades*."

"I see it. You can turn the car around while I collect my niece. I won't be long."

Josef stopped in front of the tiny antique shop which

showed a jumble of old pieces in a dusty display window and boasted an eight foot wooden wine press leaning precariously against the entrance.

"I'll turn the car up by the castle," he said. "There's a cul-de-sac nearby. Then I'll return to pick you up."

David looked inquiringly at Gail. "Do you mind waiting with Josef? I'll explain things to Pippa in the meantime."

"Of course." She peered out the car window at the shop and said dubiously, "I hope their living quarters are cleaner than the sales room."

"I hope so, too." He glanced toward the second story windows. "Well, I'll soon know. I'll be ready as soon as I can collect Pippa and her belongings."

Josef drove the car carefully up the winding street toward the castle at the top of the hill. "Would you like to get out and see how they've restored the building, Miss Alden?"

"I'd like to but I don't think we'd better take the time right now. Perhaps I can walk up here after dinner or tomorrow morning. It must be fun to spend the night in a place like that."

"Yes—but you will enjoy the *estalagem* Mr. Knight has chosen. It's very old, too." His expression was droll. "But comfortable . . . so all the Americans like it."

Gail smiled back. "Good. Frankly, I don't understand why it's necessary to skip clean towels in a hotel just for atmosphere."

His shrug was typically European. "Sometimes it's the custom. Besides, it's cheaper." He backed the car into a convenient space and cramped the steering wheel to turn back the way they'd come.

"It's a good thing this car isn't any longer," she said, admiring his dexterity.

"The streets in Obidos have atmosphere, too." He

47

sighed noisily. "Frequently I prefer the freeway going out of Lisbon."

"Never mind . . . once we pick up Mr. Knight's niece you can relax for the night." She peered out the car window. "What the dickens is happening in front of the antique shop? I think it's a fight . . ."

Her voice trailed off as they neared an angry knot of people clustered where David had entered the building. At the car's approach, they saw his tall figure break from the middle of the group and stride toward them. He had a murderous expression on his face as he opened the back door with a jerk and flung himself on the seat.

"Let's get out of here, Josef. Right now!"

The driver didn't argue. He scarcely waited for the door to close before flooring the accelerator and letting the Mercedes' powerful engine do the rest.

"What's happened?" Gail was staring through the back window at the group of sullen faces. In astonishment, she saw a thickset man shake a threatening fist at her before he got in a small black car parked by the side of the shop. She turned back to David. "Why, they're as mad as hops! And where's Pippa?"

"Gone."

"Gone!" Her voice climbed an octave. "You mean she's lost?"

"I mean that my ex-brother-in-law said to hell with visitation rights and decided he wants to keep her. Pippa's halfway back to Granada by now with her nurse."

"What was the fuss on the sidewalk then? Those people looked ready to kill you."

"They wouldn't have gone that far but they would have enjoyed riding me out of town on a rail. To them, I was a kidnapper wanting to keep Pippa from her rightful home. The nurse probably spent her time telling Ricardo's side of the story to all her relatives."

"I'll be darned. What can we do now?"

"Carry on as we planned, I guess. Josef—take us down to the inn. We'll stay there tonight."

"Very well, senhor."

"You'll have to call your sister," Gail said reflectively to David.

"Damn! I hate to. She'll really hit the ceiling."

"Wouldn't you . . . if it were *your* daughter?"

"If she were my daughter, she'd be living at home with two parents. God—what a mess."

Gail impulsively reached over and patted his hand. "It'll be all right. Pippa's father . . . Ricardo . . . surely he'll listen to reason when you see him."

"I hope so." David took a deep breath and exhaled slowly. "Well, there's no use stewing tonight. At least, Pippa's perfectly all right. She's probably delighted to be going back to her father." He looked out as the car slowed. "Here's the inn. They don't seem to bother with parking lots so we'll just have to unload in the middle of the street." He turned back to Gail with an amused expression. "At least we're far enough on the other side of town so that we won't have to worry about the nurse's relatives putting ground glass in our dinner."

Gail prepared to follow him out of the car. "Thank heaven for small favors. I'm so hungry that I probably wouldn't even notice it."

Josef had slid from the driver's seat and was back unlocking the trunk.

"We'll help with that," David told him as he bent over the neatly stacked luggage. "Do you want both of your bags, Gail?"

She walked around beside him. "No, just the bigger one. . . ." The sudden whine of a high-speed car engine interrupted her and she glanced up to see an automobile careening straight down the deserted street toward them.

"My God! . . . Look out!" David shoved her toward the inn at the same time he reached out to yank Josef from the back fender on the street side.

There was a rush of air as the dark car hurtled by, missing the rear of the Mercedes literally by inches.

Gail remembered seeing Josef cross himself as he slumped against the open trunk. David was staring after the disappearing car and muttering something remarkably profane. She looked down to find herself still clinging to David's coat sleeve with one hand and had to make a conscious effort to let him go.

"That damned fool nearly killed us . . ." David was muttering.

"I thought you said they wouldn't bother us," Gail insisted.

Josef straightened although he was considerably shaken. "Who wouldn't bother us, senhorita?" he asked sharply.

"Those relatives . . . Pippa's relatives. . . ." She shook her head. "I mean, her nurse's. There was a man in a black car by the antique shop. I saw him. He was the one who shook his fist when we drove off."

A troubled look passed over David's lean face. "That's sure being hell-bent for revenge."

Josef spoke up. "The Portuguese feel things strongly, Senhor Knight. But there is no use worrying—the moment is over." He took two of their bags from the trunk and marched into the *estalagem*.

"Well, chalk one up for Josef!" Gail said, staring after him. "That car didn't miss him by more than four inches and he just says, 'The moment is over.'" Suddenly she bent over the trunk of the car and pulled out her smaller suitcase. "I've changed my mind," she said, "I'll need this after all." Seeing David's quizzical expression, she went on to explain. "There's a bottle of tranquilizers in it and there's also a phrase book for
50

European languages. I'm going up to my room and read the chapter on 'Handy Sayings for the Traveler.' With any luck I can memorize 'Where is the nearest police station?' in Portuguese before dinner."

CHAPTER THREE

David reverted to his normally efficient manner when they entered the *estalagem*. He arranged for their morning departure and then wished Josef a pleasant evening at his lodging down the street. Once Josef did a final check of their luggage which was neatly stacked by the stairs, he nodded to them both and disappeared through the door. Outwardly, at least, he was his usual placid self.

David overlooked the effusive greeting by the young desk clerk and turned to sign the hotel register. "We'd like to go right up to our rooms, please. Is there someone to take our bags?"

"Sairtanly, senhor," the clerk replied in heavily accented English. He gave the register an uncomprehending look. "Two rooms for only two people. Is a mistake . . . yes?"

Gail felt her cheeks redden. "Here we go again," she muttered to David before walking away to study a poster at the end of the counter.

"No mistake. Two rooms," David told the man firmly, making no explanation for Pippa's absence.

Gail caught the tail end of the room clerk's pitying glance. Like the train porter, he obviously presumed she was a cast-off member of the harem. Or one who forgot to pay her dues, she decided with resignation.

"If we could go to our rooms . . ." David was saying again.

"Yes . . . yes . . . senhor. I show them to you myself. The bags will come in one minute." The clerk took two keys from a board behind the desk and came around the counter. "You will follow, p'lees." He bestowed a gold-toothed smile on Gail. "The rooms are adjoining . . . as the senhor requested in his letter."

Evidently he was assuring her not to lose heart despite her protector's apparent indifference.

The man's spirited defense of her attraction made Gail bite her lip to keep from chuckling aloud. David was affected differently; if he had been businesslike before, he was glacial now. He followed the clerk up the stairs looking as if he'd like to hurry him along by planting a swift kick where it would do the most good. Gail was left to trail along in their stormy wake.

David didn't bother to exhibit any additional amiability when they reached the door of her room. There was a terse announcement that he would meet her downstairs in an hour. Then he strode on down the hall with the now thoroughly confused desk clerk almost running to keep up.

Gail closed the bedroom door behind her and leaned against it—her shoulders shaking with helpless laughter. It served David right! He had been so logical in his plans concerning Pippa and so completely illogical when it came to traveling around Portugal accompanied only by his niece's nursemaid. It had obviously not occurred to him that hotel-keepers would put a more realistic appraisal on their appearance.

She straightened and went on into the room, her gaze resting curiously on its furnishings.

The walls were painted a Wedgewood blue which provided a tasteful frame for the scattered pieces of mahogany furniture. Gail moved over to inspect one of the twin poster beds with its white cotton bedspread.

Gingerly she sat on the edge of the mattress and found it was like resting on a cement curbing. She frowned and turned back the bedcovering only to find the thin mattress was placed over a spring made solely of knotted ropes! Her lips twitched with amusement. If the pillow were as hard as the rest of the bed, she might as well sleep on the waxed tile floor.

Absently she leaned against one of the bed posts. Immediately, the carved wooden pineapple atop it fell clattering to the floor. She reached down hastily and restored it to its perch. So much for antique beds! She'd be lucky if the whole thing didn't collapse in the middle of the night.

The sight of the door which evidently connected her room and David's made her thoughts take another tangent. She tiptoed over and gently twisted the doorknob. Locked—with no evidence of a key. Not that she had expected anything else. David was definitely not the kind of man to knock on a connecting door and beg for admittance.

She strolled over to the other side of the room and poked her head around the bathroom door. There was a spacious room beyond with *azulejos*—the colorful tiles in heavenly blue shades—used as a frieze for the white-tiled walls. Her spirits took an upward bound. Things were definitely looking more promising. She leaned over the basin to wash her hands and found that, despite the elegant plumbing fixtures, only cold water dribbled from both faucets. Reaching for the small towel on a huge chrome rack, she dried her hands and told herself there were other things beside creature comforts.

She looked at her watch and went back into the bedroom. It was a pity there wasn't more time to explore the town before dinner although the experience in the street had nipped her major exploring instincts in the bud. Idly she pushed aside the glass door which

54

opened onto a small iron balcony over the deserted street. A window box filled with ivy geraniums provided a measure of privacy from the neighboring balcony about four feet away. David's balcony, Gail thought, and she retreated hastily—unwilling to meet him just then.

Resolutely she went back to the bedroom. If she couldn't find anything else to do until dinner time, she could lie down on the bed and read.

Unfortunately even an exciting novel couldn't camouflage the bed's failings. In addition to the unyielding mattress, she discovered that it also listed perceptibly toward the hall door. Experimenting, she closed her eyes and immediately clutched the pillow to keep from sliding sideways.

She sat up abruptly. This was ridiculous—she'd try the other bed. It couldn't be worse. She was just swinging her legs to the floor when a knock sounded on the connecting door.

"Who . . . er . . . what is it?" Her voice gained strength on the second try.

"I'm going down for a drink." David still sounded aloof on the other side of the door. "Are you coming?"

"Now?" She edged up to the connecting partition.

"Certainly now. Why would I be shouting through this thing otherwise?" There came a thud at the bottom of the door to illustrate.

He was still in a temper, she decided, and found herself strangely pleased.

"Well . . . are you coming?" he asked again.

She nodded, forgetting that he couldn't see her. "Give me five minutes. I'll see you down there."

"Okay." There was the sound of retreating footsteps and then the slam of his hall door closing.

Gail smiled and headed toward her dressing table, tossing her book on the bed as she passed. The paperback struck in the middle of the mattress and gently, inexorably, slid down the sloping surface onto the tile floor.

The hotel bar was just off the lobby entrance and resembled the Black Hole of Calcutta with an intricate wrought-iron chandelier casting barely enough light to let customers stumble through the maze of four dark wood tables and perch on rigid, uncushioned stools, probably used for milking in less frivolous times.

David was crouched on one in a corner, leaning against the end of the deserted bar. Two glasses were on the table in front of him.

He made a halfhearted attempt to rise as she slid onto the stool next to his. "You're late," he accused.

Gail tried to peer at her watch in the dim light. "Not very," she told him. She pointed toward the nearest glass. "Does that belong to you or me?"

"You—if you like Scotch and soda. Me—if you don't. The gardener is also the bartender. You can ring that buzzer up there and wait—or if you're thirsty, you go haul him out of the geranium bed at the back."

Her fingers closed around the glass. "Scotch will be fine, thank you. Let's not disturb the geraniums."

This new side of David's personality flustered her slightly. She thought she'd seen them all but the laconic male so close by was disturbing. He'd changed into a yellow knit sport shirt and casual cardigan sweater. His hair was still damp from a recent combing and she noticed a slight tang of shaving lotion when she leaned forward to accept a cigarette. Her glance lingered on the strong pulse beating beside that unbuttoned shirt collar.

"What's the matter?" he asked impatiently. "Aren't you . . . ouch!"

His exclamation brought her abruptly back to the present and she saw him drop a burned-out match into the ash tray and rub his forefinger ruefully. Then he turned to her. "Look—you plan to smoke that cigarette eventually, don't you?"

"I'm sorry. Of course." This time she concentrated on the flame of a new match and told herself to disregard the strong lean fingers holding it. Resolutely she pushed back from the table and picked up her drink in self-defense. The way she was feeling, she should have a cold shower rather than an iced highball. David's intent stare made things even worse. She wondered if he felt those uneasy stirrings too.

He moved abruptly as if he'd come to a decision. "Look, Gail, it's time we stopped this ridiculous fencing. . . ."

"May I join you?" A smooth feminine voice cut in from the entrance to the bar. "It's so nice to hear an American accent that I can't resist crashing the party."

They looked up to see an attractive blonde moving toward them. David pushed upright reluctantly.

"Of course. I'm David Knight . . . this is Gail Alden."

"And I'm Vivian Donnell." She beamed on them impartially. "My brother Stan will be along in a second. He went back to get his newspaper. That's why I'm so glad to see you two—if Stan and I are alone, he ignores me completely."

Gail stared at the vision settling beside David even as he was making the appropriate response. If Vivian was ignored by her brother, surely he was the only male who followed that course of action. She was strikingly good-looking with classic features and blonde, almost-white hair pulled back in a simple chignon. The severe hairdo emphasized her smoothly tanned skin and both were shown to advantage by the deep V-neckline of her white silk shift dress. Her fingertips gleamed with a matching ivory nail polish and her lips looked soft and lustrous under a pale coloring that drew masculine attention like a magnet. It was hard to determine her age but Gail guessed close to thirty despite the taut perfection of her figure.

"I think you're sweet to take pity on me," Vivian was saying confidentially to David. "You can't imagine what it does to a woman's ego to travel with her brother."

"There's no use explaining that it works both ways. God knows I've tried." A good-looking man hesitated in the doorway and then came into the bar grinning. "No, don't get up," he instructed David as he leaned over the table to shake hands. "I'm Stan Donnell. I see you've met my sister."

"Darling—I had to do something," Vivian told him. "This is Miss Alden." She let her smile linger on Gail for a moment. "And David . . . David Knight."

Gail decided she might have been presenting royalty with that breathless pause. Turning, she found Stan pulling up a stool beside her.

"What comes before Miss Alden?" he asked.

"I beg your pardon."

"You must have a first name." He grinned again. "I have to catch up fast . . . we only have fifteen minutes until dinner."

She found his amiable insistence difficult to ignore. "It's Gail . . . and what does dinner have to do with it?"

"You don't think Vivian's the only one who's bored, do you?" He gestured toward the folded newspaper he'd put on the table. "The *Herald Tribune* doesn't hold a candle to you."

David interrupted him blandly. "The service in here is pretty slow. You have to rout out the bartender if you're thirsty."

"That's all taken care of," Stan said. "I had them put some beer in the kitchen refrigerator when we registered. They'll be bringing it along any minute. I'm surprised you pried any ice cubes out of them. They're hard to come by."

"I managed," David said laconically.

Gail watched the interchange and unconsciously compared the two men. Stan Donnell was in his early thirties and several inches shorter than David's six foot height, but he had such broad shoulders that he cut an impressive figure. Evidently his nose had been broken sometime because there was a decided hump in the middle of it which seemed to fit in with his rugged features. His hair was medium brown and curly although a short haircut discouraged that tendency. Only a slight beefiness along the jowls and under his eyes revealed a tendency toward overindulgence. Even so, his outgoing personality was hard to resist.

David felt otherwise. "Evidently you've stayed here before," he said, making an obvious effort to be civil.

"A couple of times," Stan agreed.

"My brother's staying with me for the summer," Vivian contributed. "I have a villa down in Marbella . . . that's a Mediterranean resort town on Spain's Costa del Sol," she said to Gail.

"Frankly I'd rather be back on Long Island," Stan put in. "This lolling around all the time gets mighty dull. I'm in the sales end of television at home. Did pretty well if I do say so but my doctor insisted I take the summer off. Said I'd better stop pushing myself and get my blood pressure down."

"So Stan came over to spend the summer with me," Vivian said. "Only now he's bored with Marbella and insisted we do some traveling to break the monotony. Do you know Spain?" she asked David.

"Slightly." He looked up as a white-coated waiter came in the room carrying a tray with two frosted glasses on it. "Here's your beer. Would you like anything else, Gail?" His voice softened. "You don't have to drink that concoction, you know."

"It's fine, thanks."

The waiter put down the glasses in front of the Donnells and smiled as he palmed the bill Stan gave him. He gave their table a cursory glance, stopped long enough to empty the ash tray, and then disappeared.

"To your health." Stan raised his glass.

"And yours." David hoisted his politely in return.

"Where are you off to tomorrow?" Vivian asked Gail.

"Well . . . we're going south. . . ."

"Back to Lisbon and then south to Spain," David broke in, rescuing her.

"That's a coincidence!" Stan enthused. "Any hope that you'll be down Marbella way? We'd sure like to entertain you."

"It's certainly kind of you"—David tried to put some enthusiasm in his response—"but I shouldn't think we'll get that far south."

"Yeah . . . I guess you two have your plans all made." Stan gave Gail an appreciative glance.

"Oh, no—you have the wrong idea," she cut in hastily. "I just work for Mr. Knight."

"They couldn't be interested in that," David said.

Vivian laughed. "We are—but I don't blame you for not wanting to talk about your private affairs."

The tone of her voice made Gail furious even before the words penetrated.

Stan saw possible fireworks coming and hastily unfolded his newspaper. "Well, there's not much new going on around the world. Same old stuff that we have in the headlines at home." His finger stabbed at an article on the front page. "They've something different in Lisbon, though. Somebody's walked off with one of their paintings."

Vivian allowed herself to be diverted. "I thought that just happened in Italy."

"The Italians don't have an exclusive on art heists," her brother replied.

"Who cares? Perhaps somebody wanted to stir up some excitement in this country." Her eyes flicked over to David. "Believe me, you won't find any in Obidos . . . they don't even have any sidewalks to roll up at night."

"I've had enough excitement today," Gail said thinking of their brush with terror in the street. "Frankly an early night sounds good."

"Lucky you," Vivian murmured and then turned to her brother. "What are we going to do after dinner?"

He looked up from his headline scanning. "I don't know. We can always play cards. Maybe Dave and Gail could be talked into some bridge or pinochle."

"Sorry," David said firmly. "We have to make an early start in the morning."

"Well, at least you'll join us for dinner," Vivian insisted. "We Americans have to stick together."

David thawed visibly at her soft entreaty. "We'll be glad to." Belatedly, he remembered Gail. "Isn't that right?"

Gail wished she dare refuse but one look at David's face made her say hastily, "Of course. It's the nicest offer we've had today." She neglected to mention that it was the only one, as well.

Like most Portuguese meals, dinner consisted of five courses and took nearly two hours to consume. By the fish course, Gail was tired of hearing Vivian's seductive tones. She didn't have to make small talk because the decorative blonde was devoting herself exclusively to David . . . and he certainly wasn't struggling to get out of her clutches. His face was alight with interest as they argued about nightclubs in Lisbon and beaches on the Costa del Sol.

Irritably Gail unwrapped the tissue paper covering

from her hard roll and struggled to break a piece of the crusty bread.

"Need some help?" Stan was watching her with amusement.

"No thanks . . . I've made it now." Triumphantly she displayed a bite-sized piece.

"For a minute there, I thought you were wringing its neck. You had a mighty determined look on your face." He surveyed her flushed cheeks appreciatively. "I like a woman with spirit. Why don't we go for a walk after dinner and get acquainted? Vivian doesn't need me around to hold her hand." He jerked his head toward the far side of the table. "From the way she and Dave are huddling over that menu, I think they'd like being left on their own."

For an instant Gail's lacerated pride tempted her to accept. At any other time, Stan Donnell would have been a most acceptable escort but her sense of discretion made her shake her head.

"Sorry, Stan . . . let me take a rain check. I *do* have to get up early tomorrow."

"Damn! I was afraid you'd say that. Don't think I'm giving up, though. I want your home address because I don't stay in New York all the time." His grin reappeared. "I'm going to have to enlarge my sales territory."

A sudden rumble from outside underscored his words. He glanced toward the window. "Must be thunder. Sounds as if we're building for a storm."

David had looked up at the noise too. "I'm not surprised. It's been sultry all evening."

Sultry was the way Vivian was smiling at him now, Gail decided. She pushed back her chair and stood up, unable to bear another minute of it. "If you'll excuse me . . . I won't wait for coffee. I'll probably see you all at breakfast."

"You're bound to." Vivian rested her chin in her

62

palm and bestowed a lazy feline smile. "We'll be down early. Everybody is. The beds in this place are terrible but since none of us are honeymooning—it really doesn't matter, does it?"

Gail managed to shrug. "Not to me, anyway. Good night."

Later, she found it wasn't easy to summon the proper mood for sleeping even after she'd wandered around her room and undressed. The air was oppressively heavy despite her attempts to create a breeze by opening the glass balcony door and pulling back the curtains. She washed her face in cold water and pulled on a pair of sheer shortie pajamas which raised her morale but didn't lower the room temperature.

Finally she decided to try reading for a while in the big upholstered chair. She tugged it to the end of the bed in front of the open balcony door, moved an inadequate lamp as close as she could, and settled down to her novel.

By the time she had read three chapters, the rumbles of thunder had increased in volume as the summer storm approached. Gail stirred uneasily. While she wasn't terrified of thunder, the blue-white flashes of lightning made her distinctly jumpy. She sighed. Probably it would be best to turn out the light and go to bed.

She got up to put her book away and stroll to the balcony door. For the first time, she saw the stirrings of a breeze bend the flowers in the window box. She sniffed at the fresh air eagerly and stepped out on the balcony to let the wind cool her warm skin. Suddenly realizing that the light behind her would silhouette her near-naked figure, she pulled the curtained door closed behind her and then stood in the shadows to let the glorious air flow over her.

A few seconds later, a crack of lightning cleaved the sky and, almost simultaneously, thunder vibrated the entire hillside. Before Gail could do more than stare in wonder, the rain came pouring down. The cool breeze transformed to a gusty blast driving sheets of water across the unprotected balcony.

She was drenched in an instant—even before she could turn to the door behind her. Shaking her tousled hair out of her face, she pushed at the door with her shoulder . . . and then pushed unbelievingly again.

It wouldn't move an inch!

Desperately she used both hands and shook with all her might but the door remained stubbornly in place. Overhead, thunder rumbled again and the rain flooded down in answer.

Gail clutched her arms over her chest . . . aware that the shortie pajamas were sticking to her like a second skin and a highly abbreviated one, at that. If only the bikini bottom could somehow change into a maxi skirt and the sleeveless top could become a waterproof slicker! Unfortunately her fairy godmother must have been still out to dinner because the pajamas remained stubbornly as they were; two scanty pieces of pale yellow nylon plastered against her chilled skin.

A desperate glance overhead convinced her that the storm was not moving on. At this rate, she'd be huddled out in it for hours. She peered hopefully over the balcony railing but the street below was completely deserted other than for streams of water washing over the gleaming cobblestones.

She raised her head and stared at the iron railing next to hers. There wasn't a chance of reaching it— unless she'd been Tarzan with a convenient hanging vine. A strong gust hurled the rain against her with renewed force, making her entire body tremble with the cold. She had to do something . . . and quickly!

Looking down, her glance focused on a shard of pottery which had fallen onto the balcony grating from the window box soil. With a sudden surge of hope, she bent over the flower container to see that fragments of broken flower pots were mixed carelessly in with the dirt. Her eyes narrowed in concentration for an instant. Then she scrabbled in the soil to gather a handful of the pottery pieces. Standing erect again, she let fly with the entire handful toward David's closed and darkened balcony door. If only he'd hear it over the noise of the storm!

Fortunately he did. But it was an extremely irritated man who shoved his door back and stuck out a tousled head saying, "What the devil do you think you're . . ."

The way his voice trailed off when he beheld her soaked figure would have been funny at any other time.

As it was, Gail could only plead miserably, "For heaven's sake . . . get me off of here. I can't budge my balcony door!"

"You mean you've been out there all this. . . ." Belatedly it occurred to him that this wasn't the time for a lecture. He clamped down abruptly on his tirade. "Take it easy. I'll be there in a minute."

Actually it was closer to five minutes before Gail heard him struggling with the door behind her. There was a sharp blow on the metal lock and then the glass panel slid forcefully open.

She was pulled in the room in an instant—to stand dripping on the floor like a sodden Nereid who had been unhappily transplanted from the sea.

"Oh God," she murmured, "I'm so c-c-cold." She wrapped her arms about her upper body to try to will some heat back into her shaking limbs.

"You have to dry off . . . fast!" There was decision in David's voice. "Wait until I get a towel." He strode into her bathroom and emerged with the one from the rack. "This will just get you started." Draping it around her shoulders, he said bitterly, "No use hoping for a hot bath. The clerk told me they're having trouble with the boiler. Have you something warm to change in-to . . . like a wool robe?"

65

"No . . . j-just a nylon t-t-travel one," she said through chattering teeth.

"Hell! Never mind—you can borrow this." Swiftly he reached down and undid the belt on his own terry cloth robe which he'd thrown over a pair of dark blue pajamas.

"I can't take that. . . ."

"Don't be a damned fool. Get in that bathroom and peel down." He draped the robe over her chilled arm and pushed her toward the door. "I'll go back to my room and get some more towels for you." He pulled open the hall door but stopped halfway through as if he'd been clouted over the head.

Vivian and Stan were in the middle of the hotel corridor, no doubt on the way to their own rooms. Their startled and then suddenly amused gaze made Gail realize the horrible implications of the scene.

David was frozen on the threshold. Not a calm David but a distracted man with tousled hair clad only in a rumpled pair of pajamas. As for her own condition— anyone would certainly think the worst. Gail remembered how transparent her own pajamas were and hastily draped David's robe in front of her. If only she could have stayed on that balcony a little longer.

David was obviously wishing the same thing. He straightened his shoulders with a visible effort and went on out into the corridor, pulling the door tightly closed behind him.

CHAPTER FOUR

By morning, the previous night's storm had completely disappeared. Bright sunlight played over Obidos' shops and streets in accustomed summer fashion making it hard to believe there were such things as thunder and lightning a few hours before. The soft air, newly washed by the rain, smelled as if it had been bottled especially for the new day. Otherwise, the sleepy Portuguese village had forgotten the storm as it forgot other minor annoyances over the centuries.

Gail wished she could do the same. Unfortunately the events of the night were still as brightly seared in her memory as the slashes of lightning which had ripped the dark sky.

David had returned to her room a brief ten minutes later. By then, she was decorously wrapped in his thick robe which flapped around her ankles.

When she answered his soft knock, she found him fully clad in slacks and a turtleneck sweater. He was carrying a blanket and an armful of dry towels which he thrust toward her after giving her pale face a searching look.

"Here—take one of these towels and dry your hair. Never mind . . . sit on that chair and I'll do it for you."

"You don't have to bother."

"Just sit down and stop arguing," he said wearily.

"You'll be lucky if you don't end up with double pneumonia after this outing."

"You don't get pneumonia from exposure," she replied, perching on the chair cushion. "It comes from germs or viruses." Her voice was muffled as he wielded the towel vigorously on her hair. "Or maybe it's the common cold . . ."

"That blanket will do more good around your shoulders than in your lap," he said, ignoring her nervous chatter.

"All right." She let him drape it, tent-fashion. "Thank you."

He started rubbing her hair again. "I wish to God there was some hot water in this place. Maybe I'd better rouse somebody to heat a kettle in the kitchen."

"Oh no, you don't!" She would have shot up in protest if he hadn't prevented it. "I won't have anybody else disturbed. Good heavens, it's bad enough as it is." She had trouble getting the next words out. "What did you say to Stan and Vivian?"

"Nothing." He straightened and handed her the towel. "There—your hair's almost dry now."

Automatically she put up a hand to smooth her tousled mop. "What do you mean . . . nothing?"

"Just what I said. Why should I hang around a hotel hallway in a pair of pajamas and make explanations to a couple of strangers?" He reached for a cigarette and lit it without offering the package. "Besides"—his voice was grim—"they wouldn't have believed a thing I said, anyhow."

She stood up and went over to the dressing table for her comb, still clutching the blanket around her shoulders. "That's what I was afraid of. If two people were ever guilty on circumstantial evidence—that's us. It's a good thing Pippa wasn't here." She met his glance in the mirror. "That reminds me—did you get in touch with your sister?"

He shook his head. "No luck. The storm put the telephone lines out of commission. Now I think I'll try to call Ricardo in Granada first. The less fuss about all this . . . the better."

"I see." She put the comb back on the table. "I still think I should go back to Paris. . . ."

He stared at her through the blue haze of cigarette smoke. "What brought that on?"

"You needn't get mad." Defiantly she twitched the blanket tighter. "Why should you have to pay a nurse-maid when you don't need one? None of these developments were your fault. Besides, after tonight. . . ."

"Tonight be damned!" His response was gratifyingly prompt. "So *that's* what's worrying you! Deliver me from the feminine mind."

"If you think I enjoy being stared at like a . . . a. . . ." Anger made her eyes gleam. "You know exactly what I mean."

His lips twitched. "No, tell me."

"You can go to . . ."

"Bed? Precisely what I had in mind. It would be good for you, too. I suggest you wrap that blanket around your feet until you're thoroughly warm."

"You can suggest it . . ." She began in a dangerous tone.

"Fine. I'll see if you've followed orders when I come back with your brandy."

"What brandy?"

"The stuff I'm going to get for you in the bar right now. Keep that robe on when you go to bed. With any luck, you can beat getting chilled."

"But I don't want any brandy. . . ."

He paused by the door. "And I don't want any more static. Don't forget, we're taking off early tomorrow morning."

She subsided. "Oh! Well, in that case . . ."

69

"Exactly. And may I suggest you stay away from the balcony door."

"I wouldn't go near that miserable door if it were the only way out of the Inferno and the flames were licking at my heels!"

"That's the spirit. I'll leave the brandy on your bed table if you're still brushing your teeth," he relented. "But don't be late tomorrow morning."

So here she was, Gail thought, staring in the mirror at her white face. Her luggage was ready, her lipstick on, and only two minutes until H-hour when she'd walk in the dining room to face the Donnells' smirking expressions. Her stomach muscles twisted in revolt at the thought. She couldn't . . . she simply couldn't.

By the time David knocked on the door, she had her answer ready.

"Good morning," he began.

"David . . . I'm not hungry. You go on down to breakfast and I'll have coffee up here." Her words tumbled over each other in her nervousness. "I'll be ready to go when you're finished. . . ."

"They aren't there," he cut in flatly.

"Josef can come up for my . . ." Her sentence faded away. "Are you sure?" she managed finally.

"The Donnells packed their bags in a white Jaguar a half hour ago and set off. If you'd gone out on your balcony, you'd have seen them."

"I wouldn't go on that balcony if the . . ."

"Sorry, I forgot," he said hastily. "*Now* will you come down to breakfast?"

She picked up her purse and smiled. "Yes, thanks. I'd love to."

They sat at a round table for two in a sunny corner of the hotel dining room. The breakfast coffee was a strange blend but there was certainly nothing wrong with the succulent fresh strawberries sprinkled in coarsely ground sugar.

"These are marvelous!" Gail said, halfway through a giant portion.

"I thought you'd like them." David was spreading marmalade on some hard roll. "Portuguese fruit is tremendous. Too bad there aren't any apples right now . . . they'd come in handy."

She paused with her spoon in the air. "Why apples instead of strawberries?"

"I was remembering the old saying . . . 'An apple a day . . .'!"

"But who needs a doctor?"

"From the way you sound—*you* will before the day's over. You're getting a dandy cold." He leaned back in his chair and surveyed her. "Am I right?"

She was tempted to deny his accusation but that was foiled when she had to grasp a handkerchief to smother a sneeze.

"Well?" His tone dared her to challenge.

"You could make a fortune if you hung out a shingle." She picked up her spoon again.

"I'll remember that. Do you feel up to traveling?"

"Oh, yes!" It hadn't occurred to her that he might decide she wasn't well enough to go along. She glanced anxiously across the table. "Honestly, it's just a plain old cold in the nose. I'll try to keep my germs from circulating."

"I'm not worried about that. . . ."

"Well, I am. Otherwise, I'll be fine." She took a final sip of coffee. "I'm ready to go now. Josef must be waiting for us in the lobby."

He glanced at his watch as he pushed back his chair. "I want your promise that you'll sing out if you're feeling rotten. We could have a doctor look at you when we pass through Lisbon."

"I promise but I'm sure it won't be necessary." She stood up beside him. "Will we make any stops on the way?"

"A short one at Caldas da Rainha. I want to see a man at the pottery works there and get some prices." He took her elbow as they moved toward the lobby. "They have a big open-air market in Caldas. You can wander through it while you're waiting."

Her face brightened immediately. "What do they sell?"

"Spoken like a true woman," he proclaimed, grinning. "Just about everything. Wait and see."

His words were prophetic. The open-air market at Caldas was located on a huge square in the center of town and combined all the elements of an American supermarket . . . and then some. After strolling through the good-natured crowds to look at the displays, Gail was sure the only thing missing was the kitchen sink. Probably if she'd looked more closely, she could even have found one of those.

There were colorful pyramids of fresh vegetables crowded on tables and spilling onto tiled walks. Alongside, fruits were piled in magnificent profusion with yellow and green melons ranged next to oranges and plums. In between the produce displays, sturdy Portuguese farm women offered crusty loaves of homemade bread and sweet rolls. There were other women who were selling live chickens, fresh eggs, and even a small goat tethered to a cart wheel. One ancient citizen sat hunched over a wooden crate containing three plump brown rabbits. The hares slept—blissfully unaware of their impending doom. Gail stared down at them, clutched her purse more tightly, and decided to make another circuit of the square.

She paused for some minutes at a pushcart laden with bright green Pinheiro pottery, admiring the delicate designs and shapes. Finally she purchased a spoon rest, mainly to placate the hopeful vendor who had hovered so anxiously.

Then, almost as if she couldn't help it, she walked back the way she'd come.

Josef spotted her sitting on the curb when he drove the Mercedes back to the square. He maneuvered the car behind a horse-drawn wagon and pulled up beside her.

David gave her a worried glance as he opened the rear door of the car. "You look completely bushed. Why didn't you wait in the shade at the restaurant?" He gestured toward a covey of gay umbrella tables across the street.

"I'm all right." Nervously she pushed a strand of hair from her flushed forehead. "David . . . I bought something."

"I thought you would. Hop in the car . . . you can show it to us when we stop for coffee. Josef knows a restaurant on the edge of town."

"But you don't understand"—her hand flapped toward the wooden crate beside her feet—"I bought these!"

David stared unbelievingly down at the three rabbits who peered back at him from their nest of straw. "My God!"

"I got carried away," she admitted weakly.

"So you did." His expression was difficult to read. "What kind of a future are you planning for them?"

"Good heavens—I don't know! It just seemed so awful to have them lying there . . . waiting to be somebody's dinner."

"I see." One corner of his mouth twitched slightly. "Then you weren't thinking of sending them back to Cleveland?"

"In my apartment! The manager would have a fit."

"Ummm." David scratched the side of his nose thoughtfully and looked at Josef. "Can you think of a good solution to Miss Alden's problem?"

73

"I believe so. Unless the senhorita wants her money returned?"

"Oh no!" Gail put in hastily. "All I hoped was to keep the poor rabbits out of the frying pan. Perhaps some person would adopt them. . . ."

"Under those conditions . . . most certainly." Josef picked up the crate. "I'll need a few minutes. . . ."

"Of course. Take your time," David assured him. "We'll wait in the car." He glanced at Gail. "Do you want to see who finally inherits your long-eared friends?"

"No thanks." She gave a sigh of relief as Josef disappeared in the crowd.

"Come and get in the car," he said again. "I think you could do with some rest. How's your cold?"

"Fine and dandy." She unearthed her handkerchief and dabbed at the end of her nose. "In better shape than I am, at the moment. Did you see your man at the pottery works?"

"All business accomplished. There's nothing now to keep us from pursuing Pippa to Granada."

"Will we go straight there?"

"Almost—with a small detour through the Algarve on the way."

"That's the Moorish part of Portugal, isn't it?"

He nodded. "The southern tip. There's a lot of North Africa in the architectural heritage and since Pippa's perfectly all right . . . why should I skip the trip there? I *didn't* promise Margarita I'd do that." He settled back in his corner of the car and rolled down the window. "But now I'm wondering if you feel up to such a long ride."

Poor David, thought Gail. Beset with bothersome females on all sides. Aloud, she said merely, "So long as my handkerchief holds out—don't give it another thought."

74

Josef returned to the car just then, forestalling further discussion.

"It's all taken care of," he said as he got behind the steering wheel and slammed the door. "There was a young man . . . of about seven years . . . who was very pleased to have three rabbits of his very own. He promised faithfully to care for them the rest of his life . . . and theirs."

"Wonderful! Thank you, Josef." She gave David a mischievous glance. "I promise not to be so impulsive again."

"You won't have the chance. I'll come with you after this. Who knows . . . next time they might be selling horses." He was rolling up the window as the car gathered speed but suddenly he stiffened and turned to peer through the glass behind him.

"What is it?" Gail asked.

David sat back with a sheepish expression. "Nothing—really. I thought I saw a white Jaguar parked down that side street."

"Like the one belonging to the Donnells?"

"Like one belonging to lots of people." He passed it off easily.

She wasn't diverted. "Did they say they were coming this way?"

"I don't remember asking them. Eventually they're on their way back to Spain. Vivian mentioned that they might run into us."

Gail smoothed her skirt unnecessarily. "I'll bet."

"For pete's sake—you're not going into seclusion because of that . . . episode . . . last night?"

Her upward glance caught Josef's reflection in the rear-view mirror. Obviously the less said about that "episode"—the better. Deliberately she leaned forward. "Speaking of automobiles, Josef, I meant to ask if you learned anything about that driver who tried to run us down?"

He shook his head slowly. "Nothing, senhorita. As Senhor Knight said, it was probably a relative of the child's nurse. Sometimes our people drink too much wine and do silly things. This morning he's undoubtedly nursing a sore head."

"Well, thank goodness *we're* not nursing sore heads in some hospital." She sat back. "At least we'll be putting a safe distance between us when we get down to the Algarve."

Josef agreed. "They have their own kind of trouble-makers down there."

"I don't understand. . . ."

David spoke up. "He's referring to the Algarve's turbulent history. After Alfonso the Third took it from the Moors in the thirteenth century, Portuguese kings were always given the special title of 'King of the Algarve' when they were crowned. That was in case the population had any doubts about who was top man."

Gail reached for her handkerchief again. "I hope the residents don't have any strange ideas these days."

"Don't worry, senhorita," Josef said. "Now there are so many tourists on the Algarve beaches that it's difficult to find someone who speaks Portuguese. The climate makes the area very popular."

"What's the matter with the weather right here?" She gestured toward the sun-drenched fields on either side.

"Nothing . . . during the summer months, but in the winter, it's much better down south."

"Sort of a Florida or California thing," David acknowledged. "And those Algarve beaches really are great. You'll see."

At noon, they paused for lunch at Setubal and ate in the patio of a restaurant near the center of the busy town.

"This is an important port city," Gail said, consulting a thick guidebook she had purchased, "known mainly for its fish-canning industries."

76

"Not this Sunday," Josef told her, smiling.

David had insisted that he share their meal despite Josef's inclination to disappear into an inexpensive sandwich bar down the street.

"What's happening this Sunday?" Gail asked.

"There's an important bullfight scheduled." Josef pointed to a nearby signboard. "See! That poster tells about it." He noticed her moue of displeasure. "Remember, Senhorita Alden, this is a Portuguese bullfight—we don't kill the bull. It's different from Spain."

David made a sputtering sound in his beer. "Not all that different. The bull has a rough time when the *cavalheiro*—that's the fellow who's on horseback," he explained to Gail, "puts the *bandarilhas* in him."

She shuddered. "What keeps the horse from being injured?"

"The bull's horns are padded," Josef said stiffly, his national pride at stake. "In addition to the *cavalheiro*, we have the *espadas* who fight the bull on foot. Then, at the end, when the Spanish have their 'moment of truth,' we have the *mocos de forcados*."

"Help! You've lost me there, Josef."

He smiled faintly. "The *forcados* are a team of men who come in to subdue the bull."

David nodded. "Believe it or not, they're all unpaid volunteers. When I saw a bullfight here, I couldn't decide whether they were the bravest men I'd ever seen or the biggest bunch of fools."

Josef shrugged his narrow shoulders. "It depends on how you look at things, Senhor Knight. Were you impressed?"

"We all were," David admitted. "Damned if they didn't march single file right up to the bull. The leader of the *forcados* jumped on his head and horns while the rest of the troupe piled on top of both of them. The

77

next thing you knew, the bull had tossed his head and *forcados* were slammed all over the arena."

"What happened to the leader?" Gail asked.

"The last I saw, they were carrying him out of the ring with a broken leg," David said grimly.

"I think it's just as well you won't be here on Sunday, after all," Josef told Gail.

"So do I," said David. "Considering her reaction to those rabbits at Caldas, we'd probably find her trying to lead the bull out of the ring."

"Americans just don't understand," Josef said sorrowfully.

"It works both ways." Gail glanced at David across the table. "Can you imagine trying to explain our roller derbies or log-rolling contests?"

"Never in a million years." He looked at his watch and sighed. "Time to get moving or we'll never reach our hotel by dinner time."

The drive south on that summer's afternoon was one of continuing delight. The narrow road twisted its way through cork forests and then passed on to vast stretches of olive trees whose delicate leaves cast welcome shade on the baked earth beneath. As the miles went by, the olive orchards gave way to groves of fig and almond trees planted in neat, tidy rows on the hillsides.

Overhead, cottony puffs of clouds dotted the pale blue sky. When the sun neared the horizon, the blue became deeper and more intense to eventually provide one of the most spectacular sunsets Gail had ever seen.

Emerging from their car in front of their hotel in Faro some minutes later, the coloring over the western sky made her gasp with pleasure.

"David . . . look!" She caught his arm unselfconsciously. "Isn't it fantastic!"

Even Josef paused to appreciate the spectacle before he finally moved around to the trunk for their bags.

"Then there are some things in Portugal that you like, senhorita?" he said wryly.

Gail realized that he was still smarting from her criticism of bullfighting and hastened to make amends. "Many things, Josef. So many that I couldn't begin to tell you," she said with honesty.

He looked happier as he handed their luggage to a bellman. "That's good. Tomorrow you'll notice many differences when we go into Spain. The border isn't far from here." He slammed the trunk lid back down and turned to David. "If that's all, Senhor Knight—I will see you both in the morning. Eight o'clock?"

"Eight will be fine, thanks. Good night, Josef. I hope you find a good place to stay."

The driver shrugged. "In Faro . . . there are many. It's of no importance. *Boa-noite, senhor . . . senhorita.*"

Gail watched him drive off and said, "No wonder he can't understand why we ask for rooms with an adjoining bath."

"This is no time for a philosophic discussion," David said, steering her up the steps. "I hear this hotel has a first-rate dining room and cabaret."

"Tonight, I'll settle for soap and hot water." She paused next to a poster by the elevators. "I'll read about the dancing girls and wild, wild women while you register."

"It's a deal."

He came back shortly carrying two room keys. "You're on the sixth floor and I'm on the eighth." Nodding to the bellhop who was holding the elevator door for them, he went on, "There's a view of the water on one side of the hotel. . . ."

"That's good."

"And a view of the jet airport on the other."

She made a wry face. "Not so good. Ah well, we can put cotton in our ears."

"They had a choice of rooms with balconies or

79

rooms without," David continued as the elevator started with a jolt. "I decided you could do without one tonight . . . unless you're passionately attached to them."

She struggled to keep a severe expression on her face. "Very funny. Watch out that somebody doesn't push you off yours!"

He made a clucking sound with his tongue. "Temper . . . temper. Here's your floor. I'll make a dinner reservation for eight thirty if that's all right."

"It sounds good." She hesitated as the bellman picked up her bags. "Where shall I meet you?"

"There's outdoor dining on the roof. I'll come by your room and get you." He shot an anxious look at her wan face. "Don't forget to rest a while."

"All right . . . I promise." She stepped out into the corridor. "See you later."

David's suggestion for a rest was a good one and by the time he came by to collect her for dinner, Gail felt like a new woman. From the way David scrutinized her coffee-colored lace with its flattering portrait collar and nipped-in waist, he appreciated her new look as well.

"What happened to the fugitive from the common cold I dropped here?" he asked, pretending to scan the room behind her.

"She's buried beneath a pound of makeup. That reminds me, I'd better tuck another handkerchief in my purse."

"It doesn't look like a pound of makeup," he said, pursuing the subject. "I'll admit there's a slight tinge of pink to the end of the nose. . . ."

She shooed him out the door ahead of her. "If you were a gentleman, you'd never admit it. I hope our dining room table has subdued lighting so you can't find other flaws."

As they were shown to a choice location on the rooftop, David leaned down to whisper in her ear.

"Just what you ordered—a view of the city for atmosphere and candelight to provide the romantic touch." He gestured toward the tables with their glass hurricane lanterns atop gleaming white damask cloths. Nearby, members of a three-piece combo provided music for dancing or just listening.

It was much later by the time they had finished the dessert stage of the elaborate meal and were drinking their coffee.

Gail uttered a contented sigh. "I'm stuffed . . . absolutely. They obviously haven't heard of things like the Lo-Cal plate in Portugal."

"They've probably heard of them but that's as far as it goes." David indicated the dance floor where three stout couples were performing a staid fox trot. "Take a look over there if you're talking about waistlines!"

"If I stayed here for six months, I'd be exactly the same," Gail said darkly. "You should have told me to skip the whipped cream cake."

"I *did* try to change your mind."

"Yes . . . but only to have the chocolate pastry instead." She dabbed her lips with a napkin. "It's back to black coffee for breakfast."

There was a sporadic round of applause from the patrons as a dark-haired woman dressed in a clinging black crepe dinner dress and holding a lacy black shawl about her shoulders appeared on the stage of the dance floor. Behind her, two elderly guitarists replaced the musicians who had played for dancing.

David glanced at his watch. "What d'ya know—the cabaret's right on time," he said as the guitarists launched into a complicated musical introduction.

"The singer's really beautiful," Gail whispered, "but she has such a sad face."

"All *fadistas* have sad faces—that's their stock in trade." David broke off as the woman began to sing. "I'll explain later."

81

It was fully a half hour before the singer was able to leave the stage and, even then, the audience was reluctant to let her go.

"She was wonderful," Gail enthused as the applause finally died and the combo began a brisk tango, "but I wonder why she didn't sing any happy songs. I feel as if I'd been to a movie where you weep all the way through it."

"They'd throw her out on her ear if she tried anything more cheerful. The word *fado* means fate and the *fadistas* make a career out of unhappiness. Somebody once wrote that they sing about 'love lost, illusions flown, and death too soon.'"

"No wonder I felt so sad. It was like watching the heroine on a television soap opera—all noble suffering." Gail wrinkled her brow. "Do the *fado* singers always wear black?"

"Always. *Fado* originated among the poor people and in Portugal, the women wear black shawls. Most of the *fadistas* appear in the old section of Lisbon—we were lucky to see one in Faro." He scraped back his chair. "Shall we push our luck and try the orchestra? I think that's a fox trot they're going into at the moment."

Gail felt his arms go around her as they reached the dance floor and tried to make herself relax. It was especially difficult after the highly charged, emotional music of the *fadista*. Love and passion were still in the air on the dimly lit rooftop.

Every nerve ending Gail possessed was clamoring with awareness as she danced in David's close embrace. Her hand rested lightly on the shoulder of his dark suit coat and she forced herself to concentrate on the collar of his immaculate white shirt; that way she could avoid his appraising glance which always saw far too much.

His fingers suddenly pressed hard against her back.

"Relax, Miss Alden. You're being so circumspect that you make me self-conscious."

"Sorry. I'll try to do better," she murmured.

He whirled her in an elaborate turn, gripping her tightly. She faltered for a moment in confusion and then let him mold her body against his as the music accelerated.

David made an approving noise in her ear as their steps blended in perfect unison. The lights dimmed around the dance floor while the musicians went into a slow waltz. Gail's head went forward to rest against the broad shoulder in front of her and she closed her eyes in pure contentment. She couldn't have told whether the music lasted for five minutes or ten; she only knew that she could have danced like that for the rest of the night.

David evidently felt the same way. When the medley ended he kept hold of her hand and said, "Let's go across to that roof garden over there and cool off."

Gail followed meekly, aware that she would have obliged if he had told her to walk barefooted over hot coals just then.

The garden he indicated was shrouded with shrubbery and fortunately unoccupied. She sank down on a marble bench and watched as David walked restlessly over to the balustrade.

"What do you see?" she asked, trying for a calm note. "A bird's-eye view of the Algarve?"

"Make it a bird's-eye view of the hotel parking lot." He leaned against the thick railing while he searched for his cigarettes. "Want one?" he asked, holding out the pack.

"No, thank you." She leaned back on her palms. "The air feels good. It's much warmer here in the south, isn't it?"

He gave her a derisive glance while he was using his lighter. "When in doubt for topics of conversation—

rely on the weather. Your mother would be proud of you."

She was glad that the shadows hid her hot cheeks. *Now* what had happened to make him act like this? While her comment wasn't inspired, it needn't have triggered such sarcasm. David sounded as if he were deliberately trying to pick a fight. And why did he have to stand so far away? Some couples even occupied the same marble bench on rooftop gardens.

"In fact," he was going on cynically, "you could safely say that we'll have good weather for the trip tomorrow."

"I don't know a darned thing about the weather tomorrow," she snapped, "but there's not much to say about a parking lot. Now . . . if you'll excuse me . . ."

"No, you don't!" He moved to catch her shoulder as she started to rise and pushed her firmly back down on the bench. This time he sat down beside her. "Stick around a while. At least long enough for me to make another apology," he added reluctantly.

She laughed in relief. "Don't bother . . . I'll take it as read. Now . . . if you'll excuse the expression, it *is* a lovely night. There's a different feel in the air from Obidos." She put out a restraining hand as he would have spoken. "And don't you dare mention that thunderstorm!"

"Wouldn't think of it." His slanted grin showed in the partial light. "You're just feeling the attraction of this part of the world—it's no wonder the Moors were reluctant to leave it. The real romantic history of Portugal and Spain centers around the south. Too bad we didn't stop at Silves this afternoon—that's a town a bit north of here."

"What did I miss at Silves?" she asked happily, glad to be back on a friendly basis once more.

"A charming story and a castle with a very thick wall. So thick that the Moors thought it was safe from any invading army. Unfortunately their Moorish king Aben Afan hadn't counted on his daughter falling in love with a Christian knight." David inhaled on his cigarette and glanced at Gail's intent face. "Want to hear the rest of it?" he teased.

"I'd toss you over this parapet if you tried to leave without telling me. For heaven's sake, what happened?"

"Well, the princess and her lover exchanged notes until the girl decided that letters couldn't compensate for the real thing. One evening, the knight persuaded her to meet him at the Porta da Traicao . . . the Gate of Treason. As soon as she opened the portal, the Christian forces stormed through and killed the entire Moorish garrison."

"The clods! What happened to the lovers?"

"The books don't say. There is a rumor that each year the princess reappears at the castle to sing an Arabic lament at midnight on the Feast of Saint John. But to be honest, I don't think anybody's actually seen her."

"It's a lovely story anyway," Gail watched David lean forward to extinguish his cigarette in a stone saucer filled with sand. "No wonder there's excitement in the air here."

"Other people have felt it too. Henry the Navigator stood on a cliff at Ponta de Sagres about five centuries ago and dreamed of conquest. The men who sailed under him exceeded his fondest hopes . . . Vasco da Gama, Cabral. . . ."

"And, of course, Magellan."

He nodded. "But Prince Henry's spirit was behind it all. That was a good time for the Portuguese. It was a bad time when King Sebastiao defended his kingdom against Ksar el Kebir and lost it all. And it happened right here in the Algarve. No wonder this place is called the Treasure Chest of Portugal."

Gail nodded, happy to see another side of David's personality. She'd felt an underlying current between them ever since they'd danced. That was an acknowledgment of physical desire. This meeting of the minds was another way of getting to know each other—one that was almost as exciting. Womanlike, she decided to prolong the interval.

"The Moors brought a great many treasures with them, didn't they?" she asked.

"And took just as many when they left." Deliberately he reached over and captured her hand. "Gail . . . I . . ."

She interrupted him perversely. "According to Stan Donnell, the treasures are still going over the border. It was mentioned in that newspaper article."

"I didn't realize you were so interested in Portuguese art," David said flatly as he let her hand fall back in her lap. "Shall we concentrate on Goncalves or do you want to talk about all the artists in the fifteenth and sixteenth century?"

"Who's Goncalves?"

"The fellow who's supposed to have painted the stolen work." He sounded exasperated. "The one mentioned in Donnell's paper."

"Oh, I didn't know." A telling silence followed her weak comment and she wished she'd never brought up the miserable subject. David had switched his attention to a broad-leaf plant at the end of the bench. Desperately she tried another tactic. "How do you know so much about Portuguese art?"

"I don't. All I know is what I read in the magazines and what rubbed off from listening to Margarita when she lived in Spain." He stood up. "I'm going back in to have a nightcap. Will you join me?"

He would have used the same tone of voice for Pippa, Gail decided. It was certainly not the way he'd talked to Vivian Donnell when she was hanging on his arm in Obidos.

"No, thank you," she said, after swallowing hard. "I'd better go down and get some sleep." She got up, keeping the width of the bench between them. "Thanks so much for a lovely evening. Dinner was delicious and the dancing. . . ." What *could* she say about the dancing? She wished she could tell the truth and confess, "Being in your arms was heavenly! Can't we go back in there and start again?"

"We must do it again some time," David was saying distantly as he led her to the elevator. "By the way, it will probably be more convenient if you call room service for breakfast. I'll phone from the lobby when Josef brings the car around." The elevator door opened and he saw her inside. "Good night, Gail. Sleep well," he said still in that pleasant, totally disinterested tone. Before the elevator door had closed, he was on his way back to the bar.

Gail rode down to her floor feeling like a frozen lump of despair. She stepped off into the deserted corridor but hesitated before going down the hall to her room.

Why on earth had she been such a complete idiot! She had ruthlessly killed David's tentative advances and naturally he had taken offense. No man with any sensitivity would proclaim his affection for a woman who obviously wasn't interested. It hadn't occurred to her that nervousness could pass for dislike until it was too late.

Her reflection stared back at her from the antique mirror facing the elevators. Was it too late? Surely not for something so important. When a person was in love. . . . Her thoughts exploded like a box of Roman candles at the very use of the word.

No wonder she had acted like such a ninny! There had been a definite attraction all those years ago and

David had no sooner materialized in that Paris hotel lobby than she was smitten again.

Now she could admit that it wouldn't have mattered what kind of a job he had offered; she would have followed joyfully along. Even when Pippa hadn't appeared—David was still there. And David wanted her with him.

He had felt the magic when they were dancing too. A woman could tell! Then later . . . when he was going to let her see into a corner of his heart and share the enchantment, she had turned away.

She frowned and chewed on her bottom lip. So she had turned away—so why not simply reopen negotiations. Her hand reached out for the elevator button. She'd go back up and say that she'd decided on a nightcap after all. Then somehow, she'd sink her pride and let him know how she really felt.

The elevator door slid open in front of her. She stepped in and pushed the button for the roof. While the car ascended, she checked her appearance in the tiny mirrored panel behind the controls. This was no time to have a pink nose showing! Thank heaven she had decided to come back before David had time to dwell on her peculiar behavior. The elevator shuddered to a halt and she moved out into the restaurant foyer she had left just minutes before.

She located the entrance to the bar and went over to peer uncertainly into its shadowed recesses. Surely David would be easy to find.

He was.

He was standing some twenty feet away with his back to her. Gail needn't have worried about being seen because his entire attention was on the luscious brunette who had her hands on his shoulders and was gazing soulfully up at him. Her throaty voice reached Gail easily.

"David, darling," she was saying. "Isn't this wonderful! You were absolutely right when you said we'd probably run into each other over here. Talk about small worlds!"

And talk about shopworn clichés, Gail thought spitefully as she stood glued to her spot by the door.

"Come on, sweetie. . . ." The brunette reached up and playfully pinched David's chin. "When we get our drinks, you'll have to tell me what's happening at home."

Gail couldn't hear David's murmured reply but she caught the corner of his smile as he turned obediently toward the bartender. His arm rested protectively around the brunette's waist.

Gail didn't wait for any more. In fact, she even walked down the emergency stairs for two flights so that she wouldn't be caught standing forlornly by the elevator.

By the time she reached her room, the tears were streaming down her cheeks. She slammed the door behind her and fumbled on her bureau for a handkerchief to stem the tide. Wasn't it nice that she hadn't reappeared earlier to make a complete fool of herself, she thought as she blew her nose woefully. And wasn't it great that David didn't know he'd collected another victim in between Vivian and the new brunette.

Gail wondered how many other women he'd accumulated in the three years since she'd seen him.

She sank on the edge of her bed and shook her head listlessly. So much for the Moorish love story—so much for the *fadista*'s lament. They hadn't really meant a thing to him. All she had salvaged from the experience was her unscathed pride.

But as the night passed, she didn't need anyone to tell her that her dream of happiness—like a shadowed Camelot—had disappeared completely.

And that pride, even unscathed feminine pride, made a hell of a bedfellow!

CHAPTER FIVE

By the next morning, Gail had carefully worked out what her attitude was to be. She would appear courteous, calm, and distantly friendly at all times. If David tried to take advantage of that friendliness, he'd get about as far as a newsman trying to sell a *Playboy* subscription to a board member of the YWCA.

With that resolved, she dispatched her luggage to the lobby and was waiting by the hotel entrance when Josef drove up.

"*Bom-dia*, Senhorita Alden. You are early today."

"It was too pretty a morning to sleep." There was no point in mentioning that she hadn't wasted much of the night in sleeping either.

After a quick look at her pale complexion and the dark circles under her eyes, Josef apparently figured that out for himself. "Colds in the head—they are the work of the devil. No?"

"Well, certainly something horrible." She reached in her bag for her sunglasses and slipped them on. Evidently some camouflage was indicated.

"Is Senhor Knight with you?" Josef looked around from storing her cases in the trunk.

"I haven't seen him. Perhaps you'd better call his room." She waited until the driver had disappeared into the lobby before she slid into the front seat of the car.

By the time Josef reappeared with David by his side, she was deep in a pamphlet on Spanish Andalusia.

David handed his bag to Josef and came quietly up to the side of the car beside her.

"What in hell's fire are you doing up there?" he asked grimly.

Gail clamped her jaw until she could get her words under control. Distantly friendly, she reminded herself.

"Well, I'm waiting," David said, narrowing his eyes.

"I didn't think you'd mind." She portrayed bewildered femininity. "This should be such interesting country today and it's easier to see things from the front seat. Of course, if *you'd* rather sit up here. . . ." She made motions of gathering her things together.

"Don't bother." He yanked open the back door and got in the car.

There was a pointed silence while Josef closed the door behind him and then went around to slide in the driver's seat.

Gail noted that David winced visibly when the front door slammed. Probably the deep lines around his eyes and the tautness of his jaw meant that he was suffering from the beginnings of a migraine. For an instant her conscience smote her.

"If you have a headache, you'd be better up here," she began. "There's more air and Josef can open the sunshine top. . . ."

"I am perfectly all right." David's comment translated to, "Drop dead, lady."

"But migraine can be . . ."

"I do *not* have a migraine. I have a hangover, if you must know. At three o'clock this morning I was sampling Portuguese champagne with some friends of mine in the bar and, at the moment, I hate every living, breathing thing." He pulled out his own sunglasses and shoved them on. "Now—could we get on another sub-

91

ject, Miss Alden. Unless my health has a peculiar fascination for you," he added silkily.

"I don't give a . . ." she started to say and then changed to, "Not at all." Beside her, she could see Josef trying to subdue his amusement. She added over her shoulder, "You certainly don't have to account to me for anything, Mr. Knight."

"That's a blessing." He had edged into the corner and was resting his head against the back of the seat.

"You can carouse until daylight. . . ."

"It was only three o'clock. . . ."

"And keep your own private harem if you want," she added shrewishly.

At that, his lips twitched and he inclined his head to peer solemnly over the top of his sunglasses. "Now that's something I hadn't thought of. Are you volunteering?"

"In a pig's eye, I am. . . ."

He pushed the glasses back up on his nose and sighed audibly. "That's what I gathered. It's a pity that nursery help is so specialized these days." He ignored her angry gasp and went on. "If it makes you feel any better, I wasn't spending all my time lolling around in a stupor this morning. . . ."

"I *told* you that it doesn't matter to me in the slightest how you choose to spend your time."

He ignored her angry interruption. "The hotel manager and I were having an interesting conversation about who could have rifled my room last night."

Josef uttered a shocked "Senhor!" and eased up on the accelerator. "You should have spoken before. Did they take anything of value?"

"That's the damnable part of it . . . there wasn't anything missing that I could see. They even ignored some English currency that I hadn't bothered to change."

Gail stared at both men with a puzzled frown. "Well,

for pete's sake, what are we going this way for? Aren't we going to tell the police?"

David massaged his temples wearily. "What do I say? That the hotel management should be more careful in selecting its employees? I can see them yawning now. Even the manager wasn't very impressed by my story. He probably thought I was fuzzy in the head."

Gail's feelings wavered between outraged justice and perverse pleasure that David was having to pay so dearly for his night of carousing. With his monumental headache, he was scarcely in condition to argue with the authorities.

"Besides," David was going on, "if we follow our schedule, there's no time for talking to the local constabulary. Isn't that right, Josef?"

"It would be easier without interruptions," the driver admitted. "But you must decide for yourself."

Gail stared at her hands in her lap while she waited for David's answer. Suddenly the feeling of dread that she had felt on that street in Obidos settled over her shoulders like a shroud and the sun pouring in the car window lost its warmth.

"We'll go on," David told Josef.

"Are you sure?" Gail ventured timidly. "I don't like it."

"Who the hell does." David's tone showed that he was uneasy too. "But if you don't mind, let's drop the discussion *and* the subject."

"I was just trying to help. . . ."

"Well, don't! The hotel manager 'helped' by hanging on my arm and shouting at me for thirty minutes." David shuddered. "He must have sliced garlic on his toast for breakfast. I thought my head was going to fall off." He leaned back against the seat. "So now, forget that I ever mentioned the subject. There was no real harm done and next time I'll keep my luggage locked."

He shifted his attention. "Josef, what time do we get to the border?"

"Around noon, senhor."

"Which means we'll be in Seville well before dinner. Don't forget to give Miss Alden all the travel notes on the way. Wake *me* up when we get to the ferry." He slouched in the corner, folded his arms comfortably over his chest, and closed his eyes.

When Gail glanced back five minutes later, his face had relaxed in sleep. Her lips thinned to an irritated line. Damn the man! Her concern didn't mean a thing. She turned and stared out the car window beside her. Perhaps she was being unduly sensitive. Hotel rooms had been rifled before . . . and would be again. There was no reason for her to go into a decline over it. After all, she wasn't some Victorian maiden. She rubbed the corners of her eyes behind the frame of her sunglasses. By now, her sleepless night was making itself felt in more ways than one. If she didn't take care, she'd be dosing herself with aspirin at lunch time and that wouldn't do much for her "calm and friendly" image. Not that she'd been a startling success in that line anyway. The only thing her insistence on sitting in the front seat had accomplished was to give David an unencumbered space for his morning nap. He had swatted at her verbally as he would have attacked an annoying mosquito and then obviously put her out of his mind.

"Those houses over to the right, senhorita . . ." Josef was saying softly. "You'll see they have the pepperpot chimneys peculiar to the Algarve. There are many in North Africa of the same design. Perhaps Senhor Knight has told you . . . since this is his special interest?"

"No, he hasn't said anything." She was tempted to add that Senhor Knight was concentrating on women these days rather than architecture but decided it wouldn't be prudent. Instead she stared obediently at the blocks of two-storied houses they were passing. Each stood stark in the sunlight; an exact copy of its neighbor with severe functional lines and the distinctive tall chimneys.

"These are only found near Faro," Josef added. "Soon we'll come to the luxury beach resorts. The Algarve is becoming famous for them."

"Does it bother you, Josef? Seeing the old ways change so much?"

He shrugged. "We must make a living, senhorita. Besides, it isn't only the foreigners who come here to spend holidays. Many of us from Lisbon and Oporto like Algarve sunshine in mid-winter too."

"I could use a little less of it right now," she confessed, using her guidebook as a makeshift fan. "Could we open the sunshine top for more air, please?" She gestured toward the handle on the roof of the Mercedes.

The car swerved and she gave an instinctive gasp of alarm.

Josef recovered control of the vehicle quickly. "I'm sorry, senhorita. It's impossible just now. The handle which opens the roof panel needs repair. I'll turn up the air-conditioning instead."

She started to say that she preferred fresh air but subsided as the chauffeur closed the power windows and adjusted a switch on the dashboard. Gail decided David would probably prefer cool air rather than a hot breeze blowing in the back. She glanced over her shoulder at his long, relaxed figure. He looked younger somehow—although the sunglasses had again slipped down the bridge of his nose to give him a professorial image. At least that cool glance of his was shrouded momentarily. Gail wondered if he had made plans to meet his brunette later in Spain and then gave herself a sharp mental jab for bothering about such things.

"Now that we're away from the outskirts of Faro, senhorita . . . you'll see that we still have farms and countryside." Josef was taking his guide's duties seriously. "Those orchards to the left are olives and there are orange and lemon trees on the other side of the road. Do you have them in America?"

She nodded absently. "In California."

"California. Ah, yes . . . Hollywood." He beamed.

"Well . . . sort of." She wondered how to tell him diplomatically that there were few orange groves by the Hollywood freeway and decided silence was the best policy.

The next two hours passed pleasantly with the road winding through the rich farming belt and later paralleling the beach towns with their tourist hotels and camping areas. The latter featured multicolored tents set so closely together that they resembled one long canvas caterpillar. Clotheslines loaded with swimsuits, beach towels, and blue jeans were strung between the tent ropes giving the locales a gay, carnival air. The camps were vibrating with activity even in the forenoon. Smoke streamed from the chimneys of the communal kitchens and a steady column of motor scooters buzzed noisily past them on the road. Their riders were clad only in helmets and abbreviated beach gear.

"Bikinis to the left . . . and bikinis to the right. It's Coney Island on the Fourth of July," Gail murmured, disillusioned.

"Pardon, senhorita."

"Nothing important, Josef. I was just thinking that beaches are the same the world over."

"Now, I must take your word for it. But soon"—there was an undercurrent of excitement in his voice—"soon, I'll find out for myself."

"So you're going traveling, are you?" Gail smiled at his earnest profile. "I hope you fare as well as I did."

"Thank you." He turned for an instant to beam at

her. "Soon you'll have your first look at Spain and see how it compares with my country. This is Vila Real we're approaching." He nodded toward the town in front of them.

"What's special about Vila Real?"

"There's nothing special." Josef's thin features showed amusement. "We catch our ferry here across the Guadiana River ... it's the boundary between Spain and Portugal."

"I see. Next time I'll bring an atlas and not ask so many questions. Oh ... slow down a minute, will you." She was searching on the seat beside her.

He braked reluctantly. "Something is wrong?"

"No ... it's not that." She found her camera and unzipped the case. "I want a picture of those horses pulling the wagons."

"They are very common horses, senhorita."

"But those feed bags on their noses are unique." She was busily adjusting her focus. "They look like wide-brimmed beach hats big enough to hold a five-course dinner."

"Lucky horses," came a voice from the back seat.

"Senhor Knight!" Josef glanced in the rear-view mirror. "You are awake . . . no?"

"Awake . . . yes! And starving. When do we eat?"

Gail finished taking her picture and turned to give him a reproving stare. "Josef says this is where we take the ferry."

"Isn't there a later ferry?" He sat up and ran a hand through his hair.

Josef let the car idle by the curb. "There are not many vessels on this crossing, senhor. I think we should go directly on to Spain."

"Without lunch?" David sounded appalled. "No way! I'm in a weakened condition—although the nap helped," he added candidly.

"There is a splendid place to eat in Ayamonte on the

other side," Josef put in. "After we've passed through Spanish customs, I will take you there. How does that sound?"

"As if I've just lost an argument," David said. "All right, but if you find skin and bones by the time you get there—it's because you're so happy in your work." He gestured. "To the ferry dock."

Josef accelerated obediently. "This 'skin and bones' . . . I don't understand."

David sat back. "An American expression which comes from the verb 'to eat.' You will eat, Miss Alden has eaten, I'd better eat . . . or it's skin and bones. Future, past, and imperative tense."

Seeing the driver's bewildered countenance, Gail cut in. "Pay no attention, Josef. Senhor Knight makes a joke."

"Ah!" The chauffeur smiled. "An English joke. I must remember."

"Another team heard from." David was regarding her blandly. "So you're helping me out again, Miss Alden. If the meat's tough at lunch, will you cut it for me?"

She flushed and fingered her sunglasses uneasily. "There's no need to be unpleasant. . . ."

"Why? Is it a feminine prerogative? I can't get it across to you that I *have* managed fairly successfully for some years now. . . ."

"There's *certainly* no doubt about that."

He frowned. "That has the earmarks of a nasty crack."

"Not at all. The lady looked delighted so I'd say you were very successful."

"Thanks for the testimonial but just what lady are we talking about? The one I had in mind disappeared at eleven o'clock like a frustrated Cinderella who caught an early pumpkin."

"The one I'm talking about was a brunette who got

out of the pumpkin about five minutes later," Gail said, goaded on by her anger. "Or maybe it was the fairy godmother—she was old enough!"

Annoyance warred with humor on David's face for an instant before he broke into unrestrained laughter. "So *that's* it! Look, Gail—next time you schedule a ten-rounder, would you mind letting me know who's in the main event?"

His laughter didn't help Gail's frame of mind. "It's hard to know who's going to be available," she began and then stopped as Josef pulled the Mercedes into a line of cars. "Now what?"

"This is the customs station at the Vila Real dock, senhorita. If you and Senhor Knight will give me your passports, I will arrange with the Portuguese authorities for leaving the country. Then we get on the ferry."

"Do they search our bags?" David asked, taking his passport from his coat pocket and giving it to Josef.

"It's not necessary." Josef accepted Gail's passport as well and opened his car door. "The customs men know me so this should not take long. If you'd like coffee while you're waiting, senhor, there is a small restaurant next to the customs office."

"Now you're talking," David replied, clambering out. "How about you, Cinderella?"

"No, thank you. I'll stay in the pumpkin . . . I mean, the car."

"Suit yourself."

His insouciance would have irritated any woman, Gail decided, watching him stride off beside Josef without another glance. She felt a twinge of regret as she saw the shaded tables outside the restaurant and felt the sun beating into the car.

Wearily she lowered the window beside her and took a breath of the warm fragrant air. The ferry dock at the end of the street was commonplace but the flower beds lining the sidewalks to it were truly spectacular. Scarlet cannas flanked by a low-growing blue border plant provided a splash of color while, behind the beds, a row of tall trees gave a lacy network of covering shade.

The Portuguese talent for stone mosaic design was evident in the sidewalk construction. Gray cobblestones were interspersed with black and white rocks in a pleasant, undulating pattern. With the darker patches of shade, it was particularly effective.

David would like that, Gail thought idly and then she grimaced as she remembered their last conversation.

She hadn't intended to bring her dislike out into the open. Thinking back, she realized she'd acted more like an annoyed termagant than a woman who was going to be "distantly friendly."

Gail shifted restlessly on the seat. If David suffered from any guilty pangs of conscience, he was certainly hiding them well. The man was a positive menace with anything in skirts. It was a good thing she *hadn't* accompanied him for coffee, she told herself. This way, he wouldn't be hampered if he wanted to flirt with the waitress. In the meantime, she'd simmer in the car and hope that the waitress was fat, fifty, and happily married. Hopefully her husband was the cook and hated Americans. At that pleasing thought, her expression lightened.

Even this solace was taken from her when David returned, looking cheerful and refreshed.

"Guess who I met over coffee," he said, climbing into the back seat.

"Raquel Welch . . . and she was lonely," Gail said with some bitterness.

"You're close," he said amiably, "but make it a lonely blonde. Remember Vivian? She and Stan were waiting for the ferry too. He sent along his regards. At first, he was going to walk back and deliver them personally but I said you were a little under the weather."

"Thanks a lot."

His eyebrows went up. "Aren't you? Besides, I didn't think you'd want him to see you without any lipstick." He stretched out on the seat and complacently watched her burrow into her purse for a mirror. "It didn't bother me," he went on, "but I gathered you'd want to impress Stan. Anyway, I promised we'd have dinner with them in Seville tonight. By then, you can have made running repairs."

She scowled at him before applying new lipstick. "Did anyone ever tell you that you're a . . ."

"Many times," he interrupted. "But hang in there—I like a fighting spirit."

She capped the lipstick and slammed it back in her purse. "Would it help to say that I've made other plans for dinner?"

"Not a bit. You won't have to skitter off like last night. Safety in numbers, you know."

Despite his light tone, Gail noticed that there wasn't any humor in the glance he sent her way. It bored into the front of the car with chilling directness. "I'll remember," she promised and looked down at her watch so she wouldn't have to meet that gaze any longer. "When does the next ferry arrive?"

"Any time now. From the length of the line of cars in front of us, we'll be lucky to make the second one. I understand they run small ships on this crossing. Here comes Josef—maybe he has some later information."

But Josef only repeated what David had already heard. "Soon now, senhor. You see the wheelhouse of a ferry through those trees to the right."

Gail leaned forward to peer through the windshield. "It's not a very big ferry, is it?"

Josef made an amused gesture. "It's not a very big river. We'll be across in twenty minutes."

Gail watched the boatmen secure the vessel and casually let down the wooden side barriers as a platform for the cars to use when they drove off.

"I make it twelve cars on this one." Josef counted debarking automobiles and then started tallying the vehicles waiting in line ahead of them. "We won't get on."

Gail let out a soft sigh of relief. "That's all right. Perhaps the next one will be a big ferry."

Josef turned, puzzled. "This ship *is* the big one, senhorita. The next one will be ... how do you say—for holiday crowds?"

"A relief vessel," David prompted.

"That's it." Josef started the ignition and let their car inch forward as the line moved. "Today there are many people going to Spain."

"I hope they all get there," Gail said grimly.

"That reminds me," David said. "Have we cleared Portuguese customs and immigration?"

"Certainly, senhor." Josef braked to avoid the Fiat in front of them. "I will keep the passports for the formalities on the Spanish side. All right?"

"Fine with me. How about you, Gail?" He noted that her attention had switched from the ferry to an underfed dog trotting unconcernedly by the moving cars.

"Why in the dickens don't they take care of their animals here?" she murmured. "Look at that poor little dog!"

"I am looking at him," David said, "and you can't have him. Close your eyes if you have to—but forget it." His voice softened. "He's not included on your passport picture ... remember?"

"I suppose you're right. . . ."

"I know I am. Turn around and go back to worrying about the ferry."

She gave him a reluctant smile but obediently faced
102

front again and said, "That's what I was trying to avoid. Do you see the ... vessel ... coming next?"

David smothered his laughter, knowing that without Josef at her elbow Gail's description would have been considerably less diplomatic. "Don't worry," he assured her, "we won't make this one either. There go the Donnells."

"Are they friends of yours, senhor?" Josef was watching the maneuvering at the second ferry slip.

"Acquaintances. They stayed with us in Obidos and we're joining them tonight in Seville for dinner." His forehead creased in a frown. "Looks as if we'll be third in line for the next ferry. With only a Volkswagen and a Fiat ahead of us—we should make the next crossing for sure."

When their relief ferry hove into view, David and Gail could only stare at it in patent disbelief. It had started life years ago as a fishing boat and now featured peeling red paint, a consumptive motor, and just enough room on its converted superstructure for three cars—providing two of them were midget-sized.

Gail watched a crewman casually tie up to a bollard and then throw down two planks for the first car to drive across. Her eyes swept over the boat again. "They can't be serious—what is it?"

David was reading the lettering on the stern. "The *Leaky Teaky* out of Ayamonte," he said, trying to keep a straight face.

"*Out of Luck* would be nearer the truth." She shut her eyes and reopened them. The *Leaky Teaky* was still there. Listing, admittedly, but still there. She watched the driver of the Fiat ahead of them maneuver carefully over the swirling river water on the two planks before she turned to David. "You and Josef can inch over that lumber if you want but you've just lost me," she said decisively. "I'll try the gangplank on foot."

Josef agreed. "I think you both should walk on board. Really, it is the custom here." Even he sounded slightly shaken by the task in front of him.

David didn't need further persuading. He got out with alacrity and slammed the door. "We'll see you aboard, then."

Together, they watched the car being edged down the planks with the crewmen shouting instructions and gesturing extravagantly.

"I hope to God Josef doesn't hit the accelerator instead of the brake," David muttered.

"If I were driving," Gail confessed, "we'd be spending the rest of our vacation in Portugal. I don't even like narrow mountain roads."

The Mercedes was finally berthed by the bow of the craft and they heaved a sigh of relief.

Gail followed David to the makeshift passenger gangway at the stern. "I wonder if they have any life jackets aboard."

He merely snorted and led her up the ramp. "If we sink, parts of this will float." Once on deck, he moved over to lean against a storage locker. "Besides, this tub's been afloat since Magellan's time so it should be good for one more trip."

"Probably Magellan brought his own life jacket."

"Listen—you'd be about as apt to drown in a car wash. No."—he rubbed the back of his neck reflectively—"I take that back. I had a car once that had more holes than the *Leaky Teaky* and I almost *did* drown in a car wash."

She smiled, despite herself. "Served you right."

"Anyway, this'll take your mind off being seasick."

"Hardly—on a river!" she said with scorn. "Scared to death, but not seasick."

"If we go down, I'll hang onto you by the scruff of the neck," he promised. His gaze shifted to the bow of the boat where Josef was busily shooing away a crewman who wanted to examine the Mercedes. "I guess Josef plans to stay there and ride herd on the car."

"He fusses over it all the time," Gail said.

"Well, his firm holds the drivers responsible on these trips and Josef likes his job. Apparently each driver is assigned a certain car so, in effect, the Mercedes is his baby."

They were out in the middle of the wide river and the *Leaky Teaky* wheezed steadily along despite the shifting currents. At the stern, the skipper, clad in an undershirt and torn pants, lolled back and held the vessel on course by putting one bare foot on the tiller.

Gail started to giggle. "Now *there's* a man who won't get ulcers over his job."

David grinned in response. "You're so right—but if we have many more fights like this morning, *I'll* be the one with ulcers. Now that we've a minute to ourselves, I want you to hear the whole story about last night's party. No, you don't. ..." He caught her wrist when she would have edged away. "There's no escaping."

"I'm really not interested."

"Then humor me. That brunette I met last night was the wife of a friend of mine. I've known her a long time. ..."

"So I gathered." Her tone spoke volumes. "Really, this isn't necessary. ..." Suddenly the *Leaky Teaky* hit the wake of a passing fishing boat and wallowed alarmingly. Gail lost her balance and clutched at David's sleeve for support. Automatically his arm came up and pulled her close, silencing her effectively in the middle of her protest. After a moment, the ferry resumed its lethargic course and Gail removed her nose from the comforting hollow of David's shoulder.

He watched whimsically as she pushed back her hair. "Now—where were we?" he asked.

"I was saying there's no need to tell me about your 'good friends.' "

David ignored this. "If you'd come on in—you could have met her husband."

"Her husband?"

"That's right. He joined us a little later after making a phone call to Lisbon. There was some mix-up about their hotel reservations there. You would have enjoyed meeting him . . . even if you didn't care for his wife." The last comment was laced with laughter.

"Stop it. You know that's not true." Color flared in her cheeks. "Even now you're taking unfair advantage."

"My God . . . in what way?"

She gestured weakly. "You *are* my employer."

"So?"

"It makes a difference."

"Not this morning it didn't. For a minute, I thought you'd insist that I ride in the trunk."

Her eyes sparked dangerously. "If I apologize, could we please change the subject?"

"Depends on how you apologize. How about prostrating yourself on the deck at my feet and . . . never mind." He dodged as she clenched her fist. "I'll take it for granted."

"All right, then." Her breathing had quickened and it was hard to keep her voice level. Amazingly, every symptom she had felt on the rooftop the night before had returned with a vengeance. She purposefully fixed her glance on the Spanish shore. "Is that Ayamonte ahead of us?"

"As scheduled," he chuckled. "When you run out of geography questions, we can always go back to the weather."

She ignored that and continued on her subject. "It isn't much of a town, is it?"

"The Spanish like it. For pete's sake, keep your feelings quiet until we get through immigration."

The *Leaky Teaky* had reduced speed as it approached a stubby wooden pier. Two men in greasy cotton pants and T-shirts stood ready on the dock to catch the bow and stern lines. Nearby, two officials wearing immaculate uniforms of gray khaki surveyed the ferry with surprising intentness.

"Sorry," Gail said meekly as the skipper brought his ramshackle craft alongside with amazing deftness. "Is this a 'Hear No Evil—Speak No Evil' place?"

"Not generally but Franco has had enough uprisings lately that he's careful who comes into the country."

"In that case, Ayamonte is a thing of beauty. Especially since it's on dry land and that means I can get off this"—she caught his warning eye—". . . this splendid car ferry. Do they put planks down for a gangway here or do I crawl up to the dock?"

David edged her past the ferry's engine and nodded a farewell to the skipper, who was happily uncorking a bottle of wine. They paused on the deck.

"I think the best procedure is to step up and across," David said.

"I can't. Look—I'm not being difficult." She gestured toward her hemline. "My skirt's too narrow. If I hoisted it high enough to make that jump, those two policemen would have me in for indecent exposure."

His shoulders heaved with laughter. "Okay. I'll go first and haul you up. It may be undignified but it's the only way. Josef's already in the car so he has his hands full."

David waited for a minute until the *Leaky Teaky* scraped against the side of the pilings on a swell and then jumped easily up onto the wooden pier.

"Hang on my shoulders," he instructed her as he leaned over and grasped under her arms. "Forget about your skirt. Here we go . . . up, up, and awaaaay."

She landed breathlessly against him and clung for an instant until she regained her balance.

"That wasn't so bad, was it?" He was straightening the collar on her pimento-colored pique dress. "Have you a jacket or something to go with this?"

"There's a bolero in my suitcase," she said in confusion. "Why?"

He looked embarrassed. "The Spanish are funny about women wearing sleeveless dresses." He rubbed his jaw slowly as he spoke. "It might not hurt if you could pin up that . . . er . . . front . . . another inch or so, too."

Gail gave him a stricken glance and fumbled with her V-shaped neckline. "This dress is perfectly proper. Nobody in his right mind would take offense. . . ." She saw his jaw set stubbornly and broke off to sigh. "All right, I'll unpack the bolero as soon as Josef parks the car. You make me feel like a Go-Go girl."

"I honestly don't mean to. These people are just different in the way they look at things. There's even a common saying to the effect that 'If you're not selling the merchandise . . . cover it up.' " He saw her lips thin with anger. "Damn!" he muttered. "I shouldn't have said that."

"Darned right you shouldn't have! I'm glad you chose architecture instead of the diplomatic service." Her fingers were still clutching the neckline of her dress.

He reached out and pulled her hand away. "Stop being foolish. You can use a safety pin sometime before we get to Seville. In the meantime, it's a very pretty dress and"—he broke off to smile—"frankly, I like it just the way it is."

"Well, thank you." There was a thread of amusement in her words. "I take it back . . . you are diplomatic, after all."

"And hostilities were averted. C'mon, we're blocking

traffic." He caught her hand as they threaded their way along the narrow cobblestone street, dodging men with pushcarts who thronged the middle. At the corner a fruit vendor was shouting his wares and, at his feet, two little boys wearing brief shorts were wrestling over a plastic ball.

Gail peered into a tiny food shop where cans were stacked high against the walls and cereal grains were displayed in open burlap sacks on the floor. At the rear of the store, the shopkeeper leaned on the counter and thoughtfully chewed on a toothpick.

"This is a far cry from the supermarket," Gail said to David.

"Possibly . . . but Spain's changing fast. Some of the food stores in Madrid put us to shame."

"What's behind the closed doors on all these buildings?"

"Offices, probably. If you're really curious, take a look at the brass plaques by the doorbells."

She sighed. "I'm not . . . I just wondered. It seems strange to see the closed windows and drawn curtains."

"There's nothing sinister about it. It's the climate. You know what they say about 'mad dogs and Englishmen who go out in the noonday sun.' "

"And *you* want me to wear a jacket in this weather, as well," she said ruefully. "Everybody will think I've gone out of my mind." They came alongside the Mercedes. "Where's Josef?"

"Who knows? He'll be along shortly, I suppose." David opened the rear door of the car. "Want to get in while we're waiting?"

"Yes, please." She ducked her head and stepped past him. "It's a pity we can't open the sun roof for some extra ventilation," she said, sitting down and lowering the window.

David got in beside her. "Well, why can't we?"

"Josef said it was broken . . . remember? Oh, that's

right—you were sleeping off your riotous night when I asked him earlier," she teased.

"Don't make it sound like a Roman orgy. It was a very proper and discreet party—" He broke off in mid-sentence to yawn mightily.

"About three hours too long. And that's an exact quote," she added.

"Why is it that women remember the damnedest things but nothing vital like where they parked the car a half hour before."

"I hope Josef remembers that little item." She was peeping out the window.

"Why this sudden concern for Josef?"

"He has the trunk key and I can't get in my suitcase until he reappears." She noted his perplexed frown. "I want to fix this dress."

"Oh, *that!*"

"For goodness sake, what did you think I meant?"

He held up a placating hand. "I told you to forget about it for now. You can arrive in Seville wearing a bikini if you want."

"Believe it or not, I didn't have that in mind. Now what are you laughing at?"

"It just occurred to me that we're taking extraordinarily good care of each other. This morning you were reading the riot act to me. . . ."

"And a few minutes ago you were making me feel like a scarlet woman because of a simple sailor collar," she cut in defensively.

"The top of that dress has absolutely no connection with anything designed for simple sailors," he emphasized. Then he added hastily, "For God's sake . . . forget that remark too!"

Gail collapsed with laughter. "Probably your resistance is low. Maybe some lunch will help."

"It couldn't hurt. If Josef doesn't come in a couple more minutes, we'll find a restaurant on our own."

"You've said the magic words. . . . I see our Portuguese friend coming this way." She stared down the street. "He looks cheerful so everything must be all right with Spanish customs. It seems strange we didn't even have to appear. Can you imagine trying to enter the United States by remote control this way?"

"Evidently Josef knows all the angles in Ayamonte." David leaned out the window as the driver approached. "Everything all set?"

Josef beamed and opened the car door. "I have taken care of everything, senhor. Here are your passports with the Spanish entry stamp. Now we can find that restaurant for lunch."

"Don't the officials even want to go through our luggage?" Gail asked.

"They have no interest. I told them everything was all right," Josef said simply. "I have come this way many times before so they know they can trust me." He slid under the wheel. "Shall we eat in the restaurant I mentioned?"

"By all means," David told him. "I think you're wasting your talents, though," he added as Josef started the car and pulled out into the street.

"How is that, senhor?"

"You should be working the border between East and West Germany. The tourists would love to sit in their cars while you cut the red tape there." He scratched the top of his nose. "As a matter of fact, I could have used you when I flew into Honolulu from Hong Kong last year."

Josef met his gaze in the rear-view mirror. "You had trouble?"

"Nope, but they were certainly thorough. I saw more of the inside of the customs shed than the beach at Waikiki."

Gail reached for a scarf as the breeze whipped her

hair across her face. "Maybe Josef will tell you some of his secrets at lunch."

The driver's face clouded. "Secrets, senhorita?" Then his brow cleared miraculously. "Ah . . . you're making the joke again. I have no secrets. Just the usual struggle to make a living. Life is not easy for us in my country."

David cut deftly into what threatened to be a lengthy tirade. "Then we'll have to celebrate with an especially good lunch."

Josef pursed his lips. "The food will not be unique here but tonight in Seville . . . you will eat very well. I would suggest you start with some *gazpacho*. . . ."

"That's cold cucumber and tomato soup, isn't it?" Gail queried.

He nodded. "Served *very* cold. Later you can try the *gambas*. . . . I don't know the English word. . . ."

"Prawns," David supplied. He grinned wickedly. "Or possibly the *calamares*."

"What's that?" she asked with suspicion.

"Squid. It has an extremely delicate flavor."

"I'll take your word for it," she assured him.

"No . . . Senhor Knight is right. You must try everything," Josef insisted. "Your first visit to Seville is unique."

David managed a creditable leer by waggling his eyebrows. "He's telling you to 'Live a Little.' "

She smiled automatically but lowered her glance without replying.

'Live a little,' the man said. How did you live when your heart wasn't geared for a casual romantic interlude?

She decided that men were remarkably obtuse. Some day David would discover for himself how painful a brief fling could be! In the meantime, she would cling to her "distantly friendly" guise.

Her glance flickered upward and met his warm one. Confused, she looked down again.

At this rate, she'd have to do more than cling to her cool formality. She'd have to clutch it for dear life!

CHAPTER SIX

When they arrived in Seville in late afternoon, the oppressive heat put a stop to everything but brief exchanges of conversation. Even in the outskirts of the city, the simmering temperature permeated the car's interior although the air-conditioner was working to its fullest capacity.

But nothing, Gail decided, could dull the surrounding beauty of the Andalusian capital. She sat with her nose against the glass of the car window, as entranced as an overweight matron in front of a pastry shop display.

The brilliance of the flowers clustered on the high walls in the city's residential section was breathtaking. Wrought-iron gates of marvelous intricacy provided a brief glimpse into landscaped grounds and inner patios of incredible loveliness.

"How gorgeous!" Gail breathed. "I wish we could see more of them. They don't have much on public display, do they?"

David was amused. "I told you. The Spanish are possessive and protective. They don't flaunt their possessions."

Her cheeks colored at his tacit reminder. "I was talking about their homes."

"So was I. Their attitude is the same for all their things." He shifted on the seat. "But they have a good

114

excuse for being proud here—Seville is a magnificent city."

Josef concurred. "It has a remarkable history, senhor. Did you know that Mozart chose it as the setting for *Don Giovanni* and *The Marriage of Figaro*? Not only that—the painters Velásquez and Murillo were born here. Seville has always been a center of the arts."

"The political history fills a lot of textbooks too," David said.

"Weren't the Romans part of that history?" Gail asked hesitantly. "Or do I have my places mixed?"

"You're absolutely right, senhorita," Josef said. "Julius Caesar was here in forty-five B.C. There are still many Roman ruins today."

"And in seven-twelve, the Arabs arrived," David added. "They had it in hand for five hundred years until a Castilian king took over."

Josef nodded. "Ferdinand the Third. You know your history, senhor."

"It's not hard to be interested in Seville ... especially in my line of work. An architect can learn more by spending a week here than a year in some other parts of the world."

Gail turned to face him. "Why is that?"

"Every invader left the best of him behind. From Roman bridges to the Moorish carvings in the Alcazar —it's all in Seville."

She grinned impishly. "All that, and stewed squid too." Her shoulders slumped as she leaned back against the seat. "Right now I'd trade everything for a cold shower and a pitcher full of ice water."

"Even that is possible," Josef told her. "Your hotel is right at the end of this block."

"Good Lord, it looks like a Moorish castle."

"Well, it isn't," David said more practically. "The Spaniards know what pleases the tourists, too. The

115

building's only about seventy years old but the service is a heritage from another era."

He hadn't exaggerated, Gail decided later. Their deluxe reception started from the time they were whisked through the elaborate front door by two young pages dressed in identical white uniforms. They were formally conducted to an awesome registration desk and then another page took them to the ancient grilled elevator where they were ceremoniously, if slowly, raised to the fourth floor. Still another bellman led them down a wide marble corridor which boasted a long runner of oriental carpeting in the center of it.

"Señorita Alden is in here," the young man said, pointing to an alcove shielded from the main corridor by a carved wooden screen. A small gilt coronet adorned the door above the room number. "This is one of the royal suites," he added proudly.

Gail's eyes widened in surprise and she turned to David. "What does that mean?"

"Don't take it too seriously—I doubt if the royalty did. Even before Generalisimo Franco." He plucked his key from the bellman's hand. "My room is down the hall, I think. See you later."

Despite his casual disclaimer, Gail was fascinated by the size and decor of the suite when she was ushered in. The bellman put down her luggage, accepted her tip graciously, and went on his way after closing the polished mahogany door behind him. Still enthralled, she wandered into an immense Vert Issorie marble bathroom with an old-fashioned tub on claw feet and the inevitable bidet in the corner. Going back to the hallway, she peeked into a cupboard which could have housed the wardrobe of a duchess without any trouble. There was a wooden armoire of equal size in the bedroom which looked as if it hadn't been used since the Spanish Inquisition . . . and sparingly then. A monumental mahogany bed occupied the center of the room and Gail moved closer to examine the beautifully embroidered spread and bolster pillow. Her fingers went over the fine stitching reverently. She shook her head. It was like living in a museum!

She relaxed and went to sit in a blue silk damask chair near the long windows. By leaning forward and pulling back the matching damask drape, she could look down into the parklike gardens at the rear of the hotel. A low iron grill acted as a pseudo-balcony across the bottom of the windows and she smiled in remembrance of another balcony. Tonight those windows were going to stay closed no matter what the weather!

She leaned back and closed her eyes as the absurdity of the situation hit her. What a pity she hadn't tried for a nursemaid's job before if the rewards were like this. Certainly the side benefits were far better than her position in Cleveland provided, even though Pippa wasn't along to share the bounty!

For a minute, she toyed with the idea of moving to less elegant quarters but then a delightful languor overcame her guilty conscience. She kicked off her shoes and wriggled her toes happily. Surely a nursemaid was entitled to live like a queen for one night of her life.

It was some time later that a peculiar scratching noise disturbed her nap in the chair. While she struggled to wake up, the noise was repeated and then was followed by the scrape of metal in the hallway. Still slightly befogged by sleep, she padded across the bedroom carpet in her stockinged feet to peer out into the entranceway.

She stood by the bedroom door and watched her actions repeated at the end of the hall. A shaggy gray head came cautiously around the jamb as the door swung open. The surprise that came over the elderly man's face when he saw her standing there would have been ludicrous at any other time.

The silent confrontation broke abruptly.

"What do you want?" Gail asked. "What are you doing here?"

"Dispénsame, señorita." The man's thickset body bobbed in a jerky bow and he switched to accented English. "Excuse, please. I did not mean to interrupt." He reached to close the door as he backed away.

The movement was so quick that she was reminded of a tortoise withdrawing into his shell. "Just a minute!" Her command made him hesitate, enabling her to reach the entranceway and open the door again. "Why did you come in here?"

"There was some cleaning ... they told me to get it. ..." He fumbled in the pocket of his wrinkled shirt and triumphantly produced a scrap of paper with her room number on it.

"I didn't call anyone. There's been a mistake. Did they give you a name?"

"Just the number," he insisted, lowering his head and edging away. "I check again. *Buenos tardes, señorita.*"

Gail was left staring at a deserted hallway once he shuffled into a side corridor. She glanced down uncertainly at the door beside her and then stepped back into her own hallway and shot the brass bolt on the lock. Her forehead was still furrowed in thought as she marched back to the telephone next to the bed and lifted the receiver.

"May I have the desk clerk, please?" she asked, hoping for an English-speaking operator.

"One moment ... I'll ring," came the prompt response.

There was an interval while Gail gave silent thanks for bilingual telephone people and tourist hotels. Then a masculine voice came over the wire.

"Reception. Silves here."

"This is Miss Alden in room four-twenty-two."

"Yes, Miss Alden. Can I help you?"

"I'm not sure." She gave an uneasy laugh. "There

was a man here who said he was from the laundry . . . or the cleaning department."

"Was the service unsatisfactory?"

"No, it wasn't a question of that. Actually I hadn't called him at all."

"Well, then . . . ?"

She felt an instant's sympathy for David in his discussion with the Faro hotel manager. "You don't understand," she went on doggedly. "This man just walked into my room."

The clerk's interest revived. "Without knocking, Miss Alden?"

"Oh, he knocked . . . or scratched . . . or something."

"Was he offensive in any way?"

Gail felt as if she were coming off second best on the witness stand. "He didn't do a thing," she told the clerk defensively. "But he wasn't wearing a uniform and I wasn't sure he was a legitimate member of the staff."

"The hotel's cleaning is all handled by a nearby firm," he informed her patiently. "Soiled articles are given to our bellboys or maids who put them in a central depository. Sometimes the cleaning men pick up directly from the rooms if there is a rush call. At this time in the afternoon it would be difficult to trace your man. Tomorrow morning would be better . . . although if you have no specific complaint . . ." He left the conversational ball delicately in mid-court for Gail to return.

She felt like a maiden lady caught peering hopefully under the bed before retiring. "No . . . please forget it. There wasn't any harm done. It just startled me when I noticed he wasn't wearing a hotel uniform."

"But he doesn't work for us, you see. . . ."

"I understand that . . . now." She strove for a graceful exit. "Thank you for helping. I won't bother you any longer."

"It was no trouble, Miss Alden. Be sure to call if you have any further questions. . . ."

"I will, thank you." She hung up and gave the phone a hard look. "And if you have any further questions, Miss Alden," she parroted, "the hotel will be glad to furnish the number of a good psychiatrist." She sat on the edge of the bed and sighed audibly. Keep this up and she'd be needing one. First, the near-accident in the street at Obidos and now a strange man appearing unbidden in her hotel room. Even a bookmaker would say that was stretching the long arm of coincidence a little far.

She punched the bolster pillow against the headboard and leaned against it. When you added her "coincidences" to a locked balcony in Portugal and falling in love on an Algarve rooftop, it wasn't surprising that she was acting like a witless wonder.

On an impulse, she reached for the telephone to tell David of this latest installment and then pulled her fingers away. No . . . that wouldn't do. There was no reason for adding her imaginary fears to his real worries about Margarita and her family. Her lips quirked in a derisive smile as she thought about it. If the "coincidences" persisted, they might apply for a family rate at the local psychiatrist's office.

She slid down on her pillow and decided to be sensible. A sensible woman would enjoy every minute of a paid vacation like this; she'd concentrate on sightseeing and remember that employers were only men who wrote salary checks at two-week intervals.

And if any more elderly Spaniards wandered in from the hall to collect her cleaning, she'd stop trying to find hidden meanings in their visit and simply hand them her blue dress with the soup stains on the skirt.

In the meantime . . . her thoughts slowed as her eyelids drooped . . . in the meantime, a sensible woman . . . She smiled gently and dropped off to sleep.

At dinner time, David called from the lobby on the house phone. "I hope you're ready to eat," he said without preliminaries.

"I certainly am. What's the master plan . . . would you like me to come down to the lobby or should I wait here and be collected?"

"If you're as hungry as I am, you'll want to do it the quickest possible way," he avowed. "By the time Spaniards serve dinner, I'm ready for a midnight snack."

"I cheated with some tea and sandwiches an hour or so ago," she confessed. "I thought you'd do the same."

"There wasn't time. I had to see a man so Josef drove me around to his office."

"Business until now!"

His sigh was evident even over the phone. "I told you the Spanish were on a different time schedule. Anyhow, I got the information I wanted and I've just sent Josef off for the rest of the night. He was certainly anxious to go—maybe he does have a girl friend here."

"Probably he was just starving to death like some other people I could mention," she said pointedly. "You'll waste away at this rate. Where do we meet the Donnells?"

"At the restaurant on the roof." He must have heard her quick intake of breath because he went on with some amusement, "You don't mind if we eat on another rooftop, do you?"

By then she had her voice under control. "Of course not. In this climate I can understand why people like to eat outside." She hesitated before asking, "Is this a formal occasion?"

"My wardrobe doesn't stretch that far. You'll have to settle for my wearing a clean shirt and a subdued tie. Okay?"

"Of course," she said with relief. "My wardrobe doesn't stretch very far either."

"Good. Then we'll let the Donnells dazzle us."

"That's exactly what I'm afraid of."

"Coward! I'll meet you by the elevator on the roof in five minutes. Have you remembered your room key?"

"I'm sure I put it in my purse," she said, bewildered. "At least I think I did. . . ."

"Any windows open?"

"Just one . . ." She broke off. "How did you know about the window and my key?"

"I'm psychic," he mocked. "Do you have your lipstick?"

"I'll look right now." Automatically she reached for her purse to check its contents and then stopped as she heard his chuckle. Before she could think of a sufficiently scathing comment, he had hung up.

She was still smiling at his teasing when she made a final check on her appearance in the wavy wardrobe mirror. The lace frock and matching jacket she had worn in Faro did flattering things for her complexion in Seville as well. She took a minute to dab on some Narcisse Noir perfume which she had providentially purchased in Paris and sniffed the stopper appreciatively before putting it back.

On her way to the door, she remembered that she hadn't closed her window—despite David's warning. She debated going back and then abandoned the idea. A little fresh air would be all to the good.

David was waiting by the elevator in the restaurant foyer as he promised and he was obviously pleased to see her.

"I hoped you'd wear that dress tonight. You look terrific in it!"

His admiration made her poise desert her. She smoothed her skirt unnecessarily. "You look very nice, too," she said shyly but truthfully. The tailoring of his charcoal suit was impeccable and it contrasted effectively with his pale gray shirt and matching tie. "All of a

122

sudden you look as if you'd spent the winter in Palm Springs. What did you do?"

"I transacted my business this afternoon in an open patio. It doesn't take long for me to get tanned." He reached up and rubbed the bridge of his nose gingerly. "S'matter of fact, I think I stayed out a little too long."

"If I'd done it, I'd be peeling already," she confessed.

"That's the penalty of being a redhead."

"I'm *not* a redhead. . . ."

"Within spitting distance of it, then." He transferred his attention to the hovering maître d'hôtel. "My name's Knight. We're joining Mr. Donnell."

"*Sí, Señor Knight.*" The man raised an imperious finger to a nearby attendant. "*Catorce, por favor.*" He turned back and bowed to them. "Enjoy your evening, *señor . . . señorita.*"

"Who could help it . . . in a lovely place like this," Gail murmured to David as they were led through a small forest of glass-topped iron tables already well populated with dinner patrons.

At discreet intervals, tall patio lanterns with thick candles inside provided a soft flickering light in the balmy air. A raised stage was spotlighted at the far end of the dining area, the rainbow colors giving a holiday atmosphere to the scene. Three guitarists stood in the center of the dais playing innocuous dinner music.

Gail could see the Donnells waiting at a table for four. Stan got to his feet as they approached.

"You're looking great, Gail," he said after greetings were exchanged and they were all seated. "Isn't that right, Viv?"

Vivian tore her attention from David. "Charming, Miss Alden . . . or may I call you Gail?"

"Please do."

"Good! That makes everything so much more friendly. And I *do* like your dress." Her even smile gleamed.

123

"I'm beginning to think you're one of those fortunate women who looks good in anything."

In the slight pause that followed her words, Gail decided that Vivian was referring to the last time they'd met—when the only thing noteworthy about her attire was the wholesale lack of it.

The sight of her distressed face and David's sudden scowl made Stan plunge into the conversation. "I'm certainly glad we chose this time for dinner. There's just long enough to get the food out of the way before the show starts."

Gail obediently followed his lead. "Is the entertainment good?"

"I'll say. The best troupe of flamenco dancers in Spain is appearing here now." He waited for her to look suitably impressed before going on. "Surely you've heard of Elena Rodriguez?"

"I'm afraid not. . . ."

"That's why I wanted Gail to come tonight," David announced, rallying to her aid. "Flamenco's new to her. I told her she should stop haunting museums and art galleries and see a little of modern Spain."

At that blatant falsehood, Gail buried her nose deep in the menu. She could only pray that the Donnells were as vague on Spanish antiquity as she was. Her faint hope didn't last long.

"I didn't know you were keen on Spanish art, Gail," Stan said. "What did you think of the Goyas in the Prado?"

David intercepted neatly again. "We're not visiting Madrid until after we've been down to Granada on this trip." He glanced at his menu and changed the subject. "Shall I order for you, Gail, or do you want to branch out on your own?"

She was happy to sit back. "You go ahead. I'm in your hands."

"How charming," Vivian cooed. "No wonder David

124

likes to have you along. No man could resist such flattery." She looked so charming as she said it that only another woman could recognize the acid under the words.

Gail resisted the temptation to throw something and merely smiled politely . . . but as a dining room captain came up to take their order, she studied the older woman more intently.

She was wearing a black silk chiffon dress with a halter top which left her tanned shoulders sleekly bare and tonight her jewelry consisted solely of elaborate gold pendant earrings plus a wide gold link bracelet. With her platinum hair, she would have been outstanding anywhere but in Spain where brunettes were the rule, her blonde loveliness tended to mesmerize every man within call. Why then, thought Gail, does she bother being nasty to me?

Preoccupied with her thoughts, she reached for her glass of water and had it almost to her lips before she hesitated and then put it back on the table still untouched. What *did* the books say about drinking water in Spain? Was it one of the places tourists were supposed to order bottled water and leave the tap water strictly alone? She couldn't ask and look like a bumpkin in front of Vivian.

Sighing, she pushed the water away. Maybe she was being silly, but a case of "Tourist Two-Step" was the last thing she needed right now. At least there were two waiters headed toward their table bearing tureens and china, so she wouldn't starve to death.

"You'll like this first course, Gail," Stan was saying. "They make a first-rate *gazpacho* here."

She brightened. "Cold soup certainly sounds refreshing."

"It is," David said gently. "After they pour it, they bring around a tray of other stuff to put on top."

"Like a curry," Vivian put in, "except with *gazpacho*

125

you get chopped hard-boiled egg, chopped cucumber, or pieces of tomato."

"You left out the chives and croutons," Stan said.

She shrugged. "It depends on the restaurant."

"I'm sure it will be lovely," Gail said meekly. She drew back to let the waiter put a silver tureen on the table beside her so she could admire the chilled, red soup. Her smile became fixed as she stared down into the dish. Chilled, red soup indeed . . . with at least six ice cubes floating in the middle of it! "Lovely," she repeated weakly and put out her hand once again for her water goblet. She took a quick sip of liquid and let it trickle down her parched throat. If she were going to get sick, she might as well get good and sick. Tomorrow could find David searching for a nurse to care for his nursemaid—but tonight she'd "live a little."

Between courses of the delicious dinner that followed, they danced on a tiny floor in front of the raised stage. Fortunately, the music included a good sprinkling of waltzes and fox trots as well as tangos, rumbas, and cha-cha-chas. Stan had evidently concentrated on the Latin-American dances before he left New York and when he discovered that Gail was a talented partner he led her into complicated routines that left her breathless.

"Sweetie, you're terrific!" he enthused when the music finally stopped and they were leaving the floor. "I've been looking for someone who could dance like you for years." Bending, he dropped a quick kiss on the side of her neck.

She edged away. "Stop it. Everybody will think we're part of the floor show."

He burst out laughing. "Okay, if you say so—but I still intend to cut Dave out for the rest of the night. Viv's dancing isn't all that great," he added with brotherly frankness.

Gail didn't comment and they proceeded in silence to

the table where Vivian sat alone with a discontented look on her face.

"Where's David?" Gail asked as Stan held her chair. "I thought you two were dancing."

Vivian took a cigarette from her pack on the table. "We were. Some waiter tapped him on the shoulder and said something about a *teléfono*. That was five minutes ago." She used a thin gold lighter and flicked the cover back down with a decisive snap.

"The way the telephone system works over here, it could take him that long to reach the operator," Stan said with brutal frankness. "Stop fussing—he'll be along."

There was a sudden flurry of activity on the stage. A group of musicians filed in and took their places at the back of the dais while two men positioned themselves behind spotlights in the wings.

Stan glanced at his watch. "Time for the first show." He shifted his chair to view the stage more comfortably and motioned for Gail to do the same. "You'll like the program. This Elena is really a dish."

David slid into his chair beside Gail. "Made it!"

"I thought you were going to miss the entertainment," Vivian told him. "What was so important that ..." A roll of drums cut into her words as the band blasted forth with a fanfare. She shook her head in frustration and mouthed the word "later" as she settled back to enjoy the show.

Stan's prediction was right—the dancers were terrific! From the very first number, they held the audience captive to their wild, sensual spell. The dark-haired women wore long bright satin dresses with split skirts and draped fringed shawls across their shoulders. The thin silks telegraphed every movement of their bodies just as their thick-heeled tap shoes beat out a savage message of their own. The male dancers were garbed in narrow trousers and tight, waist-length jackets which displayed their magnificent physiques. Often their white ruffled shirts were open to the waist and, after a few minutes of the strenuous dancing, perspiration made their chests gleam.

If the Portuguese *fado* portrayed gentle melancholy, the Spanish flamenco was sheer sensuality, Gail decided. At first she preferred the former, gentler music and then, despite herself, she was overcome by the rhythm, the beat, and the flaunting posturings of the dancers before her. By the time Elena Rodriquez—spectacular in red satin—had completed the final number, Gail was on her feet applauding wildly with the rest of the audience.

Noisy acclaim swept over the restaurant as the flamenco aficionados tried to keep their favorite on the stage. Finally when it became apparent by her gestures that an encore was physically impossible, the audience took their seats again and let the orchestra resume dinner dancing.

"Well, how did you like it?" Stan asked Gail. "Really something, huh?"

"Act your age, Stan," Vivian told him sharply. She added to Gail, "He'd spend the night watching flamenco if he had a chance. Or maybe I should say watching Elena Rodriquez."

"Maybe you should," her brother agreed. "What a figure!"

Vivian took her cigarettes from the table and put them in her purse. "Those gyrations are like a public orgy. Frankly the whole thing has given me a headache. I'm sure you'll excuse us. . . ."

"Damn it, Vi . . . the night's still young," Stan complained.

"You can age with it after you drive me back to our hotel," she said, sweet but implacable. Her glance rested on David and Gail. "There's no need for this to shorten your evening."

"We won't be far behind you," David said, getting to his feet.

Stan gestured for the check like a man bowing to the inevitable and casually stuffed a wad of peseta notes under the silver pepper grinder. "I'm sorry to break up the party." He grinned at David as he pushed back his chair and stood up. "Frankly I had every intention of monopolizing Gail on the dance floor for the rest of the night. I'm giving you fair warning for the next time."

"I had a few plans myself," David said, helping Vivian with her black sequined stole. His hand tightened momentarily on her shoulder. "Another time, eh?"

The woman's expression of triumph was unmistakable. She gathered her stole around her like a miser gathering his gold. "Soon, I hope." The soft words were obviously for David's ears alone.

"I'm sorry about this change in plans," Gail said stiffly as they watched the Donnells leave for the elevator. "You don't have to stick around and be polite."

"My God, don't *you* start," David said with feeling. "Obviously I had to say something to Vivian after Stan started tossing compliments at you."

"There's nothing like a brother for destroying a woman's ego," Gail admitted, "but you were certainly convincing."

"Women take things too seriously." He gestured toward the dance floor. "Have you had enough of this?"

"Whatever you say."

"Frankly I could stand some peace and quiet at this point."

She nodded and reached for her purse. "Anything we could do on the dance floor now would be an anticlimax after those entertainers. Let's go."

Once they were in the elevator, David offered a

129

suggestion. "Unless you're in a hurry to get to bed ...
how about a walk? I could manage a couple of blocks
if you could."

She pretended to consider it although her pulse had
already quickened in anticipation. "Two long blocks
... or possibly three short ones," she agreed judicious-
ly. "Will I need a coat?"

"Not unless a tornado has blown up in the last three
minutes. Seville weather just gets bearable about midnight."

They strolled through the deserted lobby and received a sleepy nod from the doorman as they went out
on the wide marble steps.

"Which way?" Gail asked, hesitating at the top.

David gestured to the left. "Over there's the Tower
of Gold and a look at the river." He reached for her
hand and pulled it through the crook of his arm. "Every tourist should see the Guadalquivir by moonlight."

"You've decreed it, I suppose." Feeling the hard
length of his body close beside her, it was difficult not
to return the pressure of his arm. Instead she forced her
fingers to rest lightly in his palm.

"I've decreed it. It sounds as if you're beginning to
understand the Spanish attitude toward life."

"What's that?"

"The male sex is really lord and master in this part
of the world." He grinned down at her. "Good thing for
American women to get a glimpse of it."

"And good for American men to remember that
they're only here a short time," she countered, wrin-
kling her nose in derision. His expression sobered as
she spoke and she slowed her steps. "What's the matter?"

"We may be here a shorter time than we'd planned.
The telephone call tonight was from my sister. ... I'd
placed it before dinner. When she heard that Ricardo
had Pippa with him, she really exploded." David
130

turned onto a sidewalk edging the gardens of the hotel. "She was leaving for Heathrow as soon as she hung up."

"The London airport? But why?"

"To catch the first plane to Spain. Hell hath no fury . . . and all that. She's going to snatch Pippa back herself. Says I'm obviously no match for Ricardo. . . ."

"And she is?"

"Well, they were married for quite a while. Once she gets to Granada we'll hear the detonation from miles away."

"What happens to us?"

His mouth looked grim. "I'd better get to Granada, too. Quickly enough to pick up the pieces."

"Poor Pippa. . . ."

"Uh-huh," he agreed with a sigh. "Poor Pippa."

They strolled in companionable silence for another block. The street lights provided enough illumination to subdue the shadows but not enough to dispel the intimacy of the quiet night. An occasional car went past on the broad *avenida* to their right and once they heard the rhythmic clip-clop of a horse pulling a tourist barouche.

Gail took a deep breath of the soft, balmy air and wished she could preserve the feeling of well-being that surrounded her. Happiness was a summer night in Seville, she decided. What a pity that Margarita hadn't been able to hold onto her happiness and her marriage. She must be remembering Spanish summer nights like this, as well.

Gail stopped in the middle of the sidewalk as a stray thought flicked through her mind. "David—if your sister will be in Granada, you won't need me."

His slow smile appeared. "I'll admit that from the way Margarita sounded, I could use a bodyguard more than a nursemaid."

"Well . . . then. . . ." She was determined to keep the

131

hurt from her voice. "I'd better make arrangements to get back to Paris."

"Look!" He grasped her elbow and started walking again. "Let's get this clear. I'm not cutting your job short just because my sister changes her plans. Who knows what she'll decide by tomorrow? Besides, I thought you wanted to go to Granada. . . ."

"I did . . . I mean, I do."

"And there's no tearing hurry for you to get back to Paris, is there?"

"You know there isn't," she admitted.

"Then stop making waves. Besides, I've gotten used to a chaperone. . . ."

"Chaperone? You mean me?"

"Certainly I do. You come in handy when people like Vivian start getting ideas."

"Thanks a lot." Her tone was wry. "If you'll remember—it's my being along that gave Vivian some of her ideas in the first place."

"I told you . . . you fuss too much."

"Well, it wasn't *you* who was caught in a soaking wet shortie pajama. I'll bet Vivian hasn't forgotten that."

"I'd put more money on the fact that Stan hasn't forgotten it." He noted her stricken look and impatiently nipped her elbow with his fingers. "Don't go into a decline about something so unimportant. The chorus line in Las Vegas featured costumes like that a good ten years ago."

"If you're trying to make me feel better, you have the wrong script. Now I *do* feel like an 'X-rated' actress."

"Well, the next feature's a travelogue—so cheer up." He steered her purposefully toward the pedestrian walk on an ancient stone bridge. "Down the river there to the right is the famous Torre de Oro . . . 'Tower of Gold' to you. It's quite a sight with those spotlights playing over it."

She stared at the round tower which looked like a

thick gold column beside the darkness of the slow-moving river. "Beautiful," she murmured. "How did it get its name in the first place?"

"There are two theories. Some people say it was because the Moors stored their treasure in it. In those days it was connected to the Alcazar ... or palace ... by a fortified wall."

"What's the other theory?"

"Much more prosaic. It was named after the gilded tiles which originally decorated the outside walls of the tower."

"And now—what's it used for?"

He drew her closer and she felt his fingers lightly explore the delicate bones of her shoulder. "Now? Nowadays it serves as an excuse for a man to take out his chaperone at midnight. It comes under the heading of 'Education,' you see, so it's quite acceptable."

Her eyes clung to his. She tried not to tremble as his hand traced upward to the tip of her ear. "Did you need an excuse?" she managed finally.

"Well, you turned down my invitation for a drink last night so that was out. I wasn't taking any chances tonight." If he felt the tremor of her response to his caresses, he was kind enough to ignore it.

There was a moment of silence while he gently tilted her chin up. Gail caught her breath and swayed toward him. His clasp tightened until their lips were just a whisper apart and then ... deliberately he let his arm drop.

He turned brusquely away from her. "We'd better get back to the hotel. It's late and we have a long drive tomorrow." His voice was rough but it wasn't giving anything away.

Gail was so astonished that she could hardly answer. Chagrin and embarrassed pride fought a losing battle as she stood there. If she could have escaped by jumping off the bridge, she would have clambered over the rail in an instant. As it was, she could only fall into step beside him and mutter, "Of course. Whatever you say."

She chewed miserably on her lower lip as they moved slowly back along the garden path. Her thoughts weren't as decorous—they raced on ahead.

What on earth had made the man change his mind so abruptly! One minute he was going to kiss her—and the next, he had drawn back as explicitly as she had in Faro. Surely he wasn't paying her back in her own coin.

She shook her head, perplexed. David couldn't have had any doubts about her response this time. It was very clear that she wouldn't have pulled away screaming if he had followed through with the kiss. Perhaps he *was* extracting a subtle revenge. Her chin lifted defiantly. Why didn't the man just slap one of those steamship labels on her—the kind that read "Not Wanted on Voyage." Then he could make everything absolutely clear.

Now she had to make it just as plain that his change of heart hadn't bothered her in the least. That she was used to men who started to make love to her and then broke off to take a walk.

Like hell she was!

She reached out and snapped off the end of a bordering vine—knowing David's stubborn neck would have afforded far greater satisfaction.

There was only one thing left to do. Somehow she had to prove that she really didn't care.

Opening her mouth, she started to talk.

All the way back to the hotel, she chattered as if she were a tour guide determined to make good. At first, David was dragooned into a long explanation of Moorish architecture. If his conversation even started to falter, she asked another question that elicited a three-minute response. He was still stumbling through an elaborate discourse on the Almohade influence in Seville when they arrived at the hotel.

"If I'd known you were so interested in my work, I'd have brought along a set of encyclopedias," he said bitterly as they went up the steps.

Secure now in the well-lighted lobby, Gail favored him with a wide-eyed stare. "I found it absolutely fascinating! Too bad it's so late or we could go into it further."

"And it's too bad there are so many people around or I could turn you over my knee and let you know what I think of *that* remark." He reached over and caught her hand. "Don't try scuttling up those stairs —we'll take the same elevator. My God, you'll have the desk clerk thinking I'm a sex fiend." He bent his head as she made an incoherent murmur of protest. "*What* did you say?"

She tugged on her fingers futilely. "If you think I'm going to tell you, you're crazy."

"Then stop struggling. What the devil's the matter with you?"

Gail was not about to admit that only one thing made a woman madder than having an unwelcome pass made at her—and that was not having any made. "There is nothing the matter," she hissed, with a bright smile for the benefit of the desk clerk. "I merely want to go to bed."

"That's where we're headed."

"Alone," she added so he wouldn't get the wrong idea.

"Oh, for God's sake . . ." he exploded and would have said more except for an interruption from the clerk.

"*Señor Knight . . . por favor!*"

They pivoted toward the reception desk.

"Yes, what is it?" David asked coldly.

"*Teléfono, señor.*" The clerk caught himself and continued in English. "It must be important, Mr. Knight. The man has called twice before."

"All right, thanks." David rubbed the side of his face wearily. "May I take it on your phone?"

135

"Of course, señor." The clerk offered the receiver.

David's grasp on Gail's hand tightened as he pulled her with him toward the desk.

"Let me go," she commanded and added more reasonably, "Please, David. I won't run away." Only then did he release her. She stood quietly at his side as he put the phone to his ear.

"Knight speaking."

Gail could tell from his expression that the call was serious. There was a penetrating masculine voice at the other end of the conversation and a rapid spate of Spanish from David in answer. By the time he hung up, all the color had drained from his face. She could hardly wait to grab his unresponsive arm and tow him across the lobby floor toward the elevator.

"What is it? Has something awful happened?"

He didn't answer but looked straight ahead like a sleepwalker.

"What is it?" she asked again. "Tell me, David."

His eyes focused on her as if he had just become aware of her presence. "The call was from the man in charge of the car rental firm where Josef works. He wanted me to know that Josef wouldn't be available to drive in the morning."

"Why not? I thought he was the permanent chauffeur for that car."

"He is . . . or was." David shook his head slightly as if to clear it. "You don't understand. Josef can't drive us because he's in critical condition in a ward at the Municipal Hospital."

Her hand flew up to her mouth. "That's awful!"

"You don't know the half of it," David told her grimly. "This wasn't an accident. Josef was beaten within an inch of his life and then left in an alley to die." His glance rested somberly on her shocked face. "I'm wondering now if we're next on the list."

CHAPTER SEVEN

It was three o'clock the next afternoon before they were able to leave Seville.

David had arranged to drive the Mercedes himself for the rest of their trip rather than hire a replacement for Josef.

"Pay attention to that city map instead of admiring the scenery," he instructed Gail as they pulled out of the circular drive of the hotel. "Spanish drivers make the Parisiennes look like a bunch of pikers—so you'll have to navigate while I try to keep us from being killed."

She winced at the expression. "Don't use that word— even in fun. After making statements to everybody and his grandmother all morning, I'm ready to have a nervous breakdown right here and now."

"Just wait until we've had a couple of 'near misses' on the road to Cordoba," he said, maneuvering past a city bus. "You'll really be ready for one, then."

"You're a cheerful soul." She peered at him over the tops of her sunglasses. "Don't look so grim—I was just fooling."

"Sorry. I guess I should be thankful that Josef is still alive. At least when he regains consciousness he'll be able to tell the police what really happened." He frowned as they approached a busy intersection. "Do

137

we turn left here or farther down the street?" There was no reply and he shot a sideways glance at her. "Wake up! You're not paying attention. Which way?"

"Oh! Just a sec. . . ." She studied the map hastily. "You don't turn for another half mile or so."

"Ummm . . . okay. What was so fascinating out the window?"

Her voice was forlorn. "A last glimpse of the Giralda Tower and the Alcazar. I wish I'd had time to see them properly. I *did* peek at Christopher Columbus' tomb in the cathedral while you were at the police station but I felt guilty about even that."

"I don't know why. Josef's getting the best of care and he couldn't have visitors in his condition. There was nothing anyone could do—even if we'd stayed in Seville. The police admitted that."

"I suppose you're right. . . ."

"I know I am. Besides, I'll call from Cordoba tonight. The police detectives promised to let me know if there were any new developments."

"I'm glad of that. Here's the turn you're looking for." She consulted the map again. "From here on, we stay on this road."

"Along with half the people in Seville." He was waiting for a break in the long line of cars.

"There's certainly more traffic here than in Portugal. If I were on the Spanish highway commission, I'd suggest a few more roads and a few less trucks," she said wryly as the Mercedes joined a lengthy string of vehicles bunched together on the winding two-lane road.

"So would I. Thank the Lord we have an air-conditioner in the car; it must be well over a hundred this afternoon."

They were rapidly clearing the outskirts of the city and getting into flat grass lands turned brown by the strong Spanish sunshine.

138

"The scenery was a lot more interesting yesterday." Gail was still wishing she could have seen Seville's famed Alcazar. When she hadn't planned to visit Spain, it hadn't seemed important. But to be a block away and miss the chance was another kettle of fish entirely.

David evidently understood how she was feeling. "Don't fret," he said in a soothing tone. "We rejoin the Guadalquivir River when we get into Cordoba and things will look better to you. A lot of people think it's one of the prettiest areas of Spain."

"I'm sure it is." She grimaced apologetically. "Sorry, I didn't mean to be a poor sport." She felt she should make amends. It certainly wasn't David's fault that their day had turned out this way. The news about Josef and the tag end of her cold were making her feel underpar physically but she needn't take her unhappiness out on David. He had enough troubles of his own. She sighed softly and tried to look on the bright side of things. At least drinking the water last night at the restaurant hadn't brought on any disastrous results.

". . . that's if you're interested in them," David was saying.

"I beg your pardon?"

He risked a glance at her despite the oil tanker which was zooming toward them. "I was telling about the mosque in Cordoba. Are you sure you feel all right?"

"Well, I'm functioning at half-speed, at least," she declared. "Tell me about the mosque again." Her lips curved upward. "This time you'll have my undivided attention."

"I'm glad I didn't insist on your trying the *sangria* at lunch if you act this way when you're cold sober." He grinned when he saw her derisive gesture from the corner of his eye. "About the famous mosque at Cordoba, madam . . . now that I have your attention. . . ."

"I'm all ears."

"There I disagree." He went on smoothly. "As I was saying . . ."

". . . before you were so rudely interrupted . . ."

"Before I was so rudely interrupted," he concurred austerely. "The mosque at Cordoba is probably the second most important Arabic building in Europe."

"So they try harder," she murmured.

"I think it was better when you weren't listening," he decided.

She grinned unrepentently. "The most important Arabic building being . . ."

"The Alhambra in Granada, naturally. Whatever do they teach women in school these days?"

"You'd be surprised. Seriously, what makes the Cordoba mosque so great?"

"For one thing, there's some Moorish fan-vaulting in a chapel that's unbelievably beautiful . . . all gold leaf and mosaic."

She let out a happy sigh. "Sounds terrific. Will we get there before closing time?"

"With any luck." He frowned as he observed the line of traffic in front of them. "And provided we don't get stuck behind any more trucks." His hand went out to the dashboard. "Shall I turn on the radio and see if I can find some music?"

"Ummm, please. It's especially nice when I can't understand the commercials."

He was fiddling with the dials. "I could translate. . . ."

"Don't you dare! I may need a tour guide but on some things—blissful ignorance is great."

The shadows cast by Cordoba's many shade trees were lengthening when the Mercedes crossed the ancient stone bridge with its Roman foundations and Moorish arches at the edge of the city.

David pushed his sunglasses up to his forehead and let the car's speed drop as he relaxed behind the wheel.

"Below us, Madam Alden—the Guadalquivir River. Ahead, the provincial capital city of Cordoba. You will note the statue of Archangel Raphael, the city's patron saint. . . ."

"I am noting. . . ."

"And beyond that, the Archbishop's palace. . . ."

"One Archbishop's palace coming up," she intoned. "You know, you could make a fortune with American Express as a courier. I hadn't realized architects were so versatile. Can you cook, too?"

"When I'm desperate. Can you?"

"I guess so," she stammered, wondering why in the dickens she'd gotten on that subject. "Is it important?"

"Don't worry." He grinned mockingly. "I won't put you to the test tonight. We're booked into the *parador* at the far edge of town."

"I wish you'd use words I could understand."

"Want it by syllables? Par-a-dor."

She shook her head. "I know how to pronounce it. What does it mean?"

"It's an inn . . . or a hotel . . . run by the Spanish government. There had just been a cancellation at this one when I called from Seville."

"Sounds great. Is that where we're going now?" she asked as he turned into a shop-lined cobblestone street winding up the hill.

"Nope. We'll take in the mosque first and work up an appetite for dinner. You might want to see some of the leather factories here, too."

Her eyes sparkled with anticipation. "If I'd known Spain had all this, I would have come years ago." She opened her purse to search for her comb. "Finding your ad in the *Herald Trib* in Paris was a stroke of pure luck!"

He pulled up behind a tour bus at the entrance to the mosque and shut off the ignition. "I feel that way too. Fate steps in at the damnedest times." The laughter

141

lines at the edge of his eyes deepened. "Makes you wonder what the elusive lady has in store next, doesn't it?" Before she had a chance to answer, he added lightly, "I'll go buy the tickets. You come along when you're ready."

The mosque was even more interesting than Gail had expected. She marveled over the eight-hundred marble columns supporting the vast interior and ogled the famous Mihrab part with its lavish gold trimmings.

"The niche faces Mecca, of course," David told her, "but in this mosque it doesn't happen to face east."

Gail stared at the magnificent mosaic encrusting the walls and ceiling with gemlike colors rich enough to satisfy an Arab sheik. "Who could possibly care," she murmured. "It's so beautiful."

He nodded. "I'm glad the Christians didn't destroy it when they came along. Their explorers weren't so charitable with the Inca and Aztec treasures." His steps slowed beside one of the striped marble columns. "You're really enjoying all this, aren't you?"

"Doesn't everyone?" Her expression turned to whimsy. "By rights, I should be paying you for letting me tag along."

"I thought we'd settled that nonsense once and for all." He urged her forward impatiently. "Come on, there's just enough time to see the main altar before they throw us out of here. It's way past closing time."

When they finally reached the curving driveway for the *parador,* it was considerably later. By then, Gail was balancing two leather pictures in her lap: tangible evidence of their visit to a Cordoban leather factory after leaving the mosque.

She eyed the modern hotel in front of them with pleasure, admiring the trim outlines of white stucco and the inevitable wrought iron balconies fronting the windows.

David evidently saw the balconies, too. "I wonder

what the weather is going to be like tonight," he muttered in an amused undertone. "Those gray clouds to the west could mean a summer storm."

She smiled. "I told you—I've learned my lesson. No more balconies for me ... even if they have a blizzard with four-foot drifts."

"Too bad." He was grinning in response as he braked in front of the entrance and turned off the ignition. "That night at Obidos wasn't all bad. There were some parts definitely worth remembering." He rested his hand lightly on her knee. "Need any help with that stuff?" He nodded toward the pictures.

"No, thanks," she said, thinking that he could change the subject quicker than any man she knew. Evidently his sentimental thoughts on Obidos were just as fleeting as his physical contacts—since his hand was now safely back on the steering wheel. She gazed moodily through the windshield.

These days with David were like one long fencing match; each had parried the other's occasional thrusts and then promptly retreated at the crucial moments. So far, the contest was a draw. Unfortunately now she didn't know whether to turn in her foil for a new match or just retire ignominiously from combat.

"Hang on. I'll come around and open your door." David got out on his side to circle the car. "Unless you want to admire those pictures tonight," he said when he had helped her out, "I'll store them in the trunk. It means one less thing to pack tomorrow."

"All right." Gail trailed him to the rear of the car. "You know, you're getting horribly efficient."

"Margarita wasn't as charitable in her choice of words. She tossed in 'stubborn,' 'hard-headed,' and 'impossible.' "

"Spoken like a true sister."

She watched him hand their bags to a waiting boy

143

and then put the pictures in the trunk. He closed the lid and tested the lock.

"You didn't take her seriously, did you?" she asked.

"Margarita? Lord, no." He reached back in the car for his sport coat and slung it around his shoulders. "You should have heard some of the things I called her in our salad days." He shook his head reminiscently. "I thought she'd mellowed since then but last night was a real throwback. I hope she cools off before she meets Ricardo." He nodded for her to precede him into the lobby. "Better get your passport out—they'll want to see it when we register."

The desk clerk welcomed them with passable English which turned to rapid Spanish when David replied in his own language. All the formalities of registration became easy and they were soon in the elevator being taken to their rooms.

As the elevator door opened on the third floor, it revealed a gleaming white corridor. The only splashes of color were in the blue and purple carpet laid down the middle of a black terrazo floor. In Gail's room, the same shades predominated on the floors and walls with the addition of warm brown in the contemporary teak furniture.

"Everything all right?" David asked, poking his head around her door as he waited for the bellman to take him to his room.

"Oh, yes." Gail glanced at her surroundings with amazement. "But I can't get over it. . . ."

"What?"

"The contrast between our Seville hotel and this. We've covered two centuries overnight."

"I hope they've worked the same miracle in the dining room. Tonight I feel like a two-inch steak with French fries."

She looked up from admiring the handwoven bedspread. "Shouldn't you be ordering suckling pig or

144

Jamon Serrano? I thought you went for the local delicacies."

"Beefsteak is international. Not that it's all that good here," he admitted frankly.

"Serves you right. Probably the poor creatures from the bull ring are getting their final revenge on mankind."

"If you keep on, I'll be ordering vegetable soup." He straightened from his relaxed position at the door. "Can you be ready to eat in a half hour?"

She nodded. "You won't forget to call Seville and find out about Josef's condition, will you? It would be nice to know whether we could possibly be involved."

"I agree. They don't have room phones here but I'll place the call with the switchboard girl at dinner time. With any luck, I can get it right through." He looked down the hall and saw the bellhop waiting by an open door near the end of the corridor. "I'd better get going. See you downstairs in a half hour."

After a shower in her modern tiled bathroom, Gail felt immeasurably refreshed. She pawed thoughtfully through the few dresses in her suitcase and wished for the umpteenth time that she had more clothes with her. David must be well acquainted with her wardrobe by now unless he was totally unaware of such things.

With a sigh, she pulled out a plain black dress and held it up. It was simply cut but the cobwebby lace bodice over the form-fitting silk slip did marvelous things for her skin and figure.

By the time she had combed her hair softly back from her face and applied lip gloss over her bright lipstick, she felt ready to face the world again. She glanced in the mirror above the dressing table as she reached for her purse. Not bad, she decided. Really not bad at all.

The look the elevator operator gave her as she rode down to the lobby confirmed her opinion. Perhaps the liberal dusting of Spanish Geranium talc had helped, she decided happily. At least it seemed appropriate in these surroundings.

David concurred as well. He took one look when they met near the door of the dining room and whistled softly. "Hey, I like it!" He bent closer. "You smell good, too. Nice and spicy—like the flower box on my balcony." Without giving her time to feel embarrassed, he gestured to the hostess waiting in the archway. "I was able to reserve a window table," he explained to Gail as they followed in her wake through the diners. "This way we'll get a view of the countryside." He waited until they were seated and exploring their menus before he added offhandedly, "It's too bad they don't serve cocktails here. You need something to cushion the shock when I tell you about my phone call to Seville."

Gail's menu flopped down to reveal her startled face. "*Now* what's happened?"

He shook his head. "Not a word until we've had some food. I've reserved one steak—shall I make it two?"

"Whatever you say." She let her glance wander toward the sideboard where their attractive waitress stood admiring David's profile. "Do you have an 'in' with the chef as well as the hostess and waitress?"

His firm mouth softened with amusement as he noted the direction of her gaze. "We'll see. If the steaks are tender—it's worth it."

"I should take the girl aside and tell her what a stubborn creature you are."

"Not until after we eat."

She smiled and toyed with a soup spoon before asking hesitantly, "At least you can tell me if Josef's better?"

"Physically . . . yes."

"What do you mean by that?"

"I'm sorry I said anything." He directed a firm look

146

her way. "Simmer down while I order. You should know by now that food is serious business over here so listen . . . and learn."

"What kind of education did you have in mind?" Gail asked after the waitress had departed with a provocative swinging of the hips. "The Spanish conversation was a total loss but I did pick up one or two other things that might come in handy. For instance, I liked the way she leaned over your shoulder to reach for the menu. Did you know that your ears turned red?"

He tried not to grin. "If you'll look through the window to the right, you'll see the mosque that we toured." Blandly he went on, "The illuminated part is the belfry."

"Similar to 'bats in the belfry,' I suppose." She picked up her spoon as an appetizing fruit cocktail was placed in front of her. "Do they have them here?"

"Have what?" He was so bewildered by her conversation that he forgot to notice the waitress when she served his cocktail. The girl shot an annoyed look at Gail and flounced off.

"Bats in their belfry," Gail persisted.

"Damned if I know. Why the sudden interest in bats?"

"I don't have one . . . really. I'd rather talk about Seville . . . phone calls to . . . and things like that."

He took a crumb of his roll and flicked it derisively across the table at her. "*That* for you, lady. I said 'later' and later it is!"

Gail glanced up to see the waitress' disapproving expression. "Now you've done it," she told David. "Throwing the food around has shattered her ideals. What do you want to bet that our steaks will be tough?"

"Nonsense. The steaks will be delicious." He took a swallow of red wine. "This stuff isn't bad either. Have you tried it?"

She dutifully followed his lead. "Very nice." There was a slight pause before she added, "If it isn't tough, it'll be cold."

"The wine?"

"The steak," she told him austerely. "I'm sorry you're so stubborn about phone calls and telling a woman what she wants to know."

"So am I," he said fervently but with a decided twinkle. "Five'll get you ten, you're wrong about the sirloin."

"You're on."

When the meat came, it was tender but only luke-warm. Since their waitress had changed to a disinter-ested sleepwalker, it wasn't surprising. David reached in his pocket and handed over ten pesetas to Gail. "I should know better than to argue with a woman," he said with the air of a man stating plain facts. "Shall I send it back to the kitchen and have it come out burned but hot?"

"Of course not." She took another bite. "Really, it tastes fine. I didn't know I was so hungry."

"Since you're being such a good sport—I'll give in," he said as he passed her a dish containing foil-wrapped butter pats. "That phone call about Josef was such a shock that I didn't quite know how to report. I still don't," he added frankly.

She pointed her steak knife at him and waggled it purposefully.

He chuckled. "I get the idea. Don't add murder to the other charges." As she looked mystified, he went on hurriedly. "I mean that the police finally got around to taking Josef's fingerprints. Do you know that we've been riding with one of the most successful and dis-cerning art thieves in Europe?"

"Josef!" Her voice cracked and she took a swallow of wine to summon it back. "You mean he stole statues . . . or pictures . . . ?"

148

"Whatever was valuable and not nailed down," he said grimly. "Sometimes even that didn't stop Josef. When the detective read me his dossier, it sounded like the plot of a television show. It's no wonder he could talk about early Spanish painters! He had his hands on a Velásquez from a private collection three years ago and the owner paid an enormous ransom to get it back. Josef got off scot-free. That was part of the deal," he added as her eyes widened.

She sat as if stunned. "I can hardly believe it. If he has all that money, why is he driving tourists around the country?"

"I can guess the answer to that. It was the perfect way to make frequent border crossings without arousing suspicion. All he had to do was carry a fake passport and make friends with the officials at the border. You saw how easily he handled our entry at Ayamonte. He was also smart enough to pick a car hire firm which handled mainly American clients. We're not the type to cause a ripple with the immigration people." David leaned back in his chair. "Want some more coffee?"

"No, thank you." She pushed her cup and saucer to one side. "Exactly how much did Josef confess?"

"Not any more than he had to. The police got most of this information from his record. Josef regained consciousness just long enough to confirm their suspicions and admit some of his gang had given him the beating. Probably he tried to demand a bigger cut or hold out on them."

"Hold out what?" She wrinkled her nose in protest. "You're going too fast for me."

He hitched his chair forward. "This latest haul," he explained. "Remember that newspaper we saw in Obidos? It told about it."

"Stan's newspaper?"

"That's right. One of the articles mentioned the theft

of a Goncalves from the Lisbon Museum. I mentioned it in Faro—doesn't it ring a bell?"

"Not even a buzzer. I wouldn't recognize Goncalves if he came up and bit me."

"That's not apt to happen," he said dryly. "The man's been dead since the fifteenth century."

Gail looked suitably impressed. "I'm sorry to be so ignorant. Was he terrifically good?"

"The Portuguese think so." David poured another half cup of coffee for himself. "While he isn't in a class with DaVinci or Raphael, he's close enough for his paintings to be worth thousands of dollars. Even if this stolen work isn't a genuine Goncalves, it would attract plenty of collectors who have more money than morals."

Gail sat back to let a busboy clear the dishes in front of her. She waited until he moved away before asking, "Where on earth did Josef hide it?"

"As the Australians say, I haven't a clue. What's more to the point—neither do the Spanish police nor anyone else. Josef simply isn't talking at this stage. When the questioning really got interesting, he lapsed back into unconsciousness."

"I'll be darned. . . ."

"The detective put it more strongly than that," he told her. "He also wanted to be reassured that we didn't have any old masterpieces in our suitcases. Thank God I could claim Ricardo as a character reference. If my ex-brother-in-law didn't travel in the right circles, we might be returning to Seville for more questioning tonight."

"It's all right for you," Gail said soberly, "but what about me?"

"You're under my protection." He was laughing at her again. "There's no use looking so irate—this is Spain and the Women's Lib movement doesn't have a toehold yet."

She fixed him with a frosty stare. "Have you ever heard that splendid old Spanish proverb 'Hell will never be full till you be in it'?"

"Never," he said solemnly. "I must ask Ricardo. Incidentally I meant to point out that tower down in the valley . . . over there to the left. That's where they hang the women of the town who are disrespectful of male authority."

Her mouth dropped. "I don't believe you!"

He grinned. "I don't either—but it's not a bad idea, is it?"

"Idiot!" Her lips twitched in an unwilling smile. "All right, then—I'll admit that masculine protection comes in handy in this case. You're sure that I'm not a member of the gang?"

"Well, if you're carrying any old masterpieces around with you, they must be well hidden," he said, signing their dinner check. He kept his eyes averted as he added, "There certainly isn't any room under that dress you're wearing."

Her cheeks flamed. "*Now* what have I done wrong? You can't accuse me of a low neckline this time." She rang her fingers around the cowl collar which clung just off her shoulders.

He stood up and uttered a curt laugh. "There's not a thing wrong with it . . . except that you look like a sexy wench in anything you put on. If you want to know, I've had a hell of a time keeping my mind on food." He steered her toward the dining room door.

For the life of her, Gail couldn't think of an adequate reply. Fortunately David didn't seem to expect one.

When they reached the lobby, he merely said, "I'm going to try and call Margarita now. Maybe we can have a liqueur or something when I'm finished." His glance swept over her warmly. "Okay?"

"Oh, yes." She had trouble even getting those two words out coherently.

"Good." He pushed her gently toward the elevator. "I'll come up to your room and get you as soon as I'm finished."

It was all she could do to keep from saying "Don't be long" as she watched him cross the lobby. Fortunately no one could guess the way her heart was pounding as she stepped in the elevator but she bestowed a smile of such unadulterated joy on the teen-aged operator that he remembered it for the rest of the night.

Once inside her door, she whirled into an ecstatic waltz step through the hallway and into the bedroom itself. Wonderful, wonderful Spain! Wonderful, wonderful day! Absolutely the best day of her life! And from the way David had looked . . . plus the intimacy of his voice, it was certain that he felt the same way!

She tossed her purse on the bed and changed to a tango step as she hummed, "The rain in Spain stays mainly on the pla-in. . . ."

"Ole! Ole!" came a masculine voice from the doorway. "Could you use a partner?"

Gail froze in mid-step. "Stan!" She stared at his laughing face. "How did you get here?"

"The same way you did. I was just going down to dinner when I saw you duck in here. You left your door ajar or I would have knocked." He advanced into the bedroom, looking dapper in a dark blue blazer and gray slacks. "Incidentally, the door's still open so you don't have to worry about proprieties."

"I wasn't thinking of that." She pushed back a strand of hair. "You just surprised me, that's all."

He grinned and held out his arms invitingly. "You could improve on that tango with a partner. Let's take it again from the top."

She hesitated for a second before obediently moving in front of him. "What about music?"

152

"We'll try a duet . . . you can come in on the chorus. Ready?" He hummed a bar of the introduction and then swept her into an intricate tango that took them around the room and through the furniture. Gail started to giggle as she joined the lyrics of the chorus and they finished with an exaggerated Valentino swoop.

She struggled upright, breathless and laughing. "That was marvelous!" she told him. "You should stay in Spain . . . they don't have tangos like that at home."

He caught her hands and kissed them in florid continental fashion. "Der credit is for mine partner . . . she iss everytink," he said with a ridiculous German accent. "Now—we go downstairs and do eet wiz ze moosic—no?"

"We go downstairs . . . no! Oh Lord, you have me doing it," she accused, pulling her hands away. "I'm sorry, Stan. I've made other plans."

"Knight?" His thick brows came down in irritation. "I might have guessed."

She let that pass. "Where's Vivian?"

"Doing her own thing." He heard the cool note in her voice and made an effort to recapture their lighthearted mood. "Actually she stopped over to visit some friends. That's another reason I don't want to miss this chance of spending some time alone with you." Gently he grasped her shoulders and pulled her toward him. "Come on, Gail—take pity on me tonight." Without waiting for a response, he bent his head and covered her mouth with his. She was held tightly against his broad chest as the insistent kiss went on and on.

As soon as she recovered from her surprise, she struggled to free her hands and push against his shoulders. Turning her head, she gasped, "Stan, stop it! Let go of me—right now!"

"Ah . . . Gail . . . have a heart."

"Let go, I said!" Her words were accompanied by a particularly hard shove. While it didn't move his rock-like stance, it did serve to propel her backward as he reluctantly loosened his clasp. She felt the pull of material on her back as something ripped noisily.

"What *are* you doing?" She bit out the words in anger.

"Damned if I know." He was honestly puzzled. "My sleeve button's caught. Stand still or you'll make it worse." He peered over her shoulder gingerly. "Hell! It's tangled in that lace on your dress."

"Well, untangle it!"

"I'm trying. There are some knotted threads. . . ." He shook his head. "It's no use. I'll just have to yank. . . ." There was another ripping sound which made her gasp.

She surveyed the side of her bodice where the lace now hung limply from a gaping silk slip. "That's torn it," she murmured, "literally and figuratively."

"God, I didn't mean. . . ." Stan's voice trailed off and he reached up to scratch his head awkwardly. "I sure am sorry. Maybe you can find somebody in the hotel to fix it."

"I'll see." Gail managed to smile as she spoke. There was no point in telling him that the fragile lace bodice had been damaged far beyond simple repairs by a seamstress. At least she could mend the slip herself. "You'd better go so I can change," she said, pushing him toward the door. "I look like the cover illustration on a confession magazine."

"You won't let this make any difference, will you?" Stan went reluctantly into the hall. "I want to get to know you better." He stopped by the partly open door and reached for her hand. "We can take it slow and easy."

"I certainly hope so." She kept her tone light as she

eased her hand out of his grip. "My wardrobe is definitely limited on this trip."

"You know I didn't mean that. Once we get to Granada, though, we'll go shopping and get you fixed up. All the good Madrid stores have branches there."

"And *you* know I didn't mean *that*." Gail's patience was wearing thin. She reached for the door and pulled it all the way open. "I can't make any definite plans now. Let's leave it at that, shall we?"

His expression hardened. "Don't try to foist me off, Gail. I'll wait until Granada but then I'll be in touch." He bent down, kissed her roughly and then disappeared into the hall corridor.

Well! Gail let out her breath with a sigh of relief. Thank heavens that episode was over—but what a strange attitude for Stan to take. He had evidently seen through her attempt to let him down gently and was having none of it. Her lips tightened in annoyance as she turned back toward her bedroom. That was a complication she hadn't dreamed of. It was strange too, how their paths kept crossing . . . or perhaps not so strange when she remembered how Americans flocked to the same hotels abroad.

There was a brisk rap on the hall door. Stan again, no doubt. What could he have in mind this time?

Deciding to get rid of him in short order, she marched back to the hall and yanked open the door. "*Now* what? Oh!"

David was standing there, staring down the hallway to his right. "Was that Stan Donnell I saw coming out of here a minute . . ." His words stopped as he turned his head and got his first glimpse of her disheveled state. Slowly . . . deliberately . . . he ushered her back into her room and closed the door behind him. His jaw tightened as his eyes played over her torn dress in a way that made Gail turn pale. Finally his flintlike glance met hers. "So it *was* Stan?" He shoved his hands in his pockets and went on before she could reply. "What a fool I was to think you'd changed! It's the same scene, the same dialogue as three years ago, isn't it? Only the faces are different."

His searing sarcasm made Gail stop clutching the torn remnants of her dress. She felt her nails bruise her palms instead. "So you did remember me? I thought you might . . ."

"My God, yes." He uttered a brief, mirthless laugh. "You're the kind of woman that's hard to forget, Miss Alden. I even went down to that dean's office the next day to find out all about you. His secretary told me that you were practically engaged to some professor so I gave up. I thought I'd put you out of my mind completely until I received your letter of application in Paris. Then I couldn't wait to see you again."

Gail made an involuntary gesture toward him but shrank back as his glance raked her distastefully.

"David . . . please listen. I wondered about you, too. I even looked you up in the alumni files." Her words tumbled out. "The secretary gave you the wrong information. I wasn't engaged to anybody . . . ever."

"That makes it worse, doesn't it?" There was an impersonal finality in his tone. "Actually I'd given you the benefit of the doubt until now. I thought I'd made a mistake that night . . . that I'd misjudged you and I shouldn't have said what I did." He shrugged and turned toward the door. "Well, we live and learn."

"David!" she wailed. "You're not going . . ."

He looked over his shoulder. "Why not? Or are you holding an Open House tonight?" His sarcasm was fast giving way to a flaming anger. "One appearance like that is a mistake, lady. Twice it's a habit."

"You can't mean that!"

He ignored her shocked protest and went cruelly on. "Maybe you're trying for a third 'go-round' . . . without even repairing the damage."

156

"Why you . . . you sadist! How dare you say such things!" Stung to an absolute fury, she reached out and slapped him as hard as she could.

There was a moment of shocked silence. Then her palm dropped limply to her side and they stared at each other in an atmosphere so thick with emotion that it was almost visible.

David took a deep breath and let it out slowly. "Just what the hell do you think you're playing at?" he demanded ominously as she backed away from him.

Despite her lingering anger, she couldn't force herself to look at that patch of reddened skin on his cheek. Her voice wobbled defiantly. "It's all right for you to say every horrible thing that comes into your mind. I'm supposed to stand here and take it."

"Trust a woman to twist the rules. I was telling the truth. Now do you expect me to apologize for misjudging you and turn the other cheek?" He reached out suddenly to clamp onto her wrists. "Think again, lady."

She forgot her damaged dress as she struggled to free her hands. "You *did* misjudge me. I can get Stan to prove it this time. . . ."

"As if I'd listen to him!" His mouth slanted derisively.

"Why not? Don't you believe anyone?" Tears glistened in her eyes but she blinked rapidly to keep them from overflowing. "You aren't satisfied with just accusing people—you have to act as jury and then pass sentence, too. I was guilty three years ago according to your reasoning so I'm guilty now."

"If evidence counts for anything, you're guilty, all right." His cynical glance flashed over her torn frock. "Do you deny Donnell did that?"

"I'm not denying anything." Despair settled over her like a shroud but she tilted her chin defiantly. "As far as I'm concerned, the case is closed." She went on, "If you want to tilt at any more windmills tonight, Don Quixote, find yourself another battleground. I'm tired. You can leave anytime . . . but the sooner the better . . . and lock the door behind you."

As her studied insolence registered, David's face drained of color. "Not so fast," he said softly, transferring her wrists to one of his hands and grasping her chin with the other. "You're the woman who shares her wealth, remember?" His eyes narrowed. "And to think I was being gentle with you last night because I didn't want to frighten you off. You must have gotten a kick out of that." He pulled her closer. "Well, we won't miss any more fun. . . ."

She tried to shake off his fingers. "Go find yourself another playmate, Mr. Knight. Now, let me go!"

"Just as soon as I get my share of the bounty," he drawled. "Every pirate has to expect that . . . even one like you." The last was murmured against her lips as his mouth ruthlessly covered hers.

Sometime during the course of that long kiss, David released her wrists to slide his arms around her waist. His strong hands left a trail of fire in their knowledge-able wanderings and when he finally raised his head, she was too unnerved to pull away.

His heart was pounding under her fingers but her own heart was raising such a furor that she scarcely noticed it. She felt a whisper-soft movement in her hair and instinctively burrowed closer against his shoulder.

Above her head, David wore an equally dazed expression. The punishment he had devised had gotten completely out of hand somewhere in the middle of that kiss. He frowned as he tried to concentrate but concentration was difficult when a man was holding an armful of soft, fragrant femininity.

Still bewildered, he took a step backward.

Gail felt his arms slacken and, with the move, his last ill-chosen words came surging back in her memory.

So David regarded her as part of the spoils, did he? And from the way he had embraced her, caressed her . . . he was evidently expecting a lion's share.

Her eyes darkened with anger as she impulsively dodged past him in the hallway and pulled open the door.

Instinct made her want to clutch the fragments of her bodice frayed even further in that last embrace but she willed her hands to stay at her side as she faced David. "You can go now," she told him coldly. "You've had your fun and no matter what you think—this is as far as it goes. Tonight or ever," she added for good measure.

He moved slowly over to stand beside her at the open door. "I think we should go a bit further tonight," he said unevenly.

She felt a surge of elation through her body. So she wasn't the only one having trouble with her breathing after that kiss! David would have to learn to control his emotions as well as his temper.

"I'm not going anywhere," she said, deliberately misunderstanding him. "This time, the verdict is mine, Mr. Knight. But I could suggest a good spot for you. As far as I'm concerned, you can go straight to . . ."

The door slammed shut behind him before she finished the sentence.

CHAPTER EIGHT

It took her only about two minutes to decide that she never wanted to see her employer again. She'd had it!

Gail made the momentous decision as she searched through her suitcase for a handkerchief to stem the flood of tears which persisted in pouring down her cheeks. Once she had made up her mind, there was no great feeling of relief. Instead the tears flowed harder until she finally fled into the bathroom to wash her face and blot her pink and swollen eyelids with a towel. When she had finished, a look in the mirror at her torn dress and ravaged features was enough to start the deluge all over again.

She mopped up a second time, felt for the side zipper on her skirt, and let the dress fall on the tile floor at her feet. Stooping, she bundled it carelessly and then threw it into a nearby wastebasket. At least that was one part of the evening she'd never have to see again! She blew her nose disconsolately and padded back to her suitcase to look for another dress.

Her hands paused in the middle of unpacking a knitted skirt.

How could David have said such dreadful things! Any man should have the decency to ask for an explanation if he cared about a woman at all. She nibbled absently on her thumbnail as she thought it over. Caring was the operative word and it could mean different things to different people. Or different things to a man and a woman.

Slowly she drew the green pleated skirt over her hips.

It wasn't love David displayed in that kiss. Desire . . . passion . . . physical attraction . . . definitely! She couldn't deny that.

But love? Hardly.

She reached for a knitted pullover top and put her arms in the sleeves. Staying around David to let him play with her emotions made about as much sense as a nearsighted animal trainer crawling into the tigers' cage without his glasses. The results would be disastrous in both cases!

She shook her head dispiritedly. There was really only one solution.

She moved over to the dressing table and ran a comb through her hair before gathering up her cosmetics and putting them in the plastic bag in her suitcase. Fortunately she hadn't bothered to unpack more than the merest essentials before dinner so she could leave right away.

Then the enormity of her decision struck and she sank onto the edge of the bed. How in the dickens was she going to leave and where was she going if she did? Her forehead wrinkled as she scowled and tried to concentrate. Certainly her Spanish wasn't good enough to probe the mysteries of a railroad ticket office at midnight. That only left the Mercedes. She felt a momentary twinge at leaving David without transportation but he could rent a car in the morning.

She stood then and finished packing her case. If she used the car, she'd have to take it to Granada and somehow get it delivered to Pippa's house. After that, she could wash her hands of the entire Knight family!

She snapped the locks on her suitcase and put it by the door. Her camel's hair coat was thrown hastily around her shoulders as she made a last-minute check of the room. The untouched and inviting bed triggered some regret but, at the moment, sleep was the furthest thing from her mind.

At least she wouldn't have time to think about David when she was driving. Her subconscious raised its head at that declaration and pointed out that she'd have plenty of time to think about him in the next year or so. She battened down on that possibility immediately and, picking up her suitcase, went stealthily out into the deserted corridor.

Luck was with her when she made her way to the reception desk without encountering either David or Stan. Telling the clerk that she was leaving and wanted Señor Knight's car brought around proved more difficult.

"But, Señorita Alden . . . the automobile is parked for the night." He gestured unhappily in the general direction of the hotel parking lot.

"That's all right. There's no need to bother anyone. If you'll just let me have the car keys, I can manage by myself." She was sweetly insistent. "And may I have my passport, please?"

He handed it over with reluctance. Although clearly mystified by her change of plans, he was so used to dealing with eccentric travelers that he wasn't especially suspicious. "You are not sleeping in your room? Then you won't be here for breakfast service."

"No—I'll be in Granada by then . . . at the home of Señor Knight's sister," she said, crossing her fingers. "Naturally I'll pay for my room now," she added hastily.

He surveyed the registration book and looked still more puzzled. "But that is not necessary—Señor Knight has paid everything."

"I see." She was disconcerted to learn that she was indebted to David still further but she managed an

162

artificial smile. "Well, that takes care of everything, I guess. If I can have the keys for the car. . . ."

Turning, he fished them out of the pigeonhole for David's room but hesitated before handing them over. "Señor Knight does not need the car tonight?"

"Certainly not." She took a gamble. "Call him and check if you'd like. . . ."

"There is no telephone in his room, señorita."

"Of course—I'd forgotten." She looked around the deserted lobby. "Perhaps someone could go up and ask. . . ."

"No, that is not necessary." He blinked solemnly and told himself there were limits to a man's responsibility. Besides, his dinner was getting cold in the kitchen. He gave her the keys without further question. "The car is just beyond the door. Have a pleasant trip, Señorita Alden. *Buenas noches.*"

"*Gracias. Buenas noches, señor,*" she responded, using four words of her ten word Spanish vocabulary.

Trying to look casual, she strolled out to the parking lot but once next to the Mercedes she unlocked it hastily and dumped her suitcase in the rear seat. She put the key in the ignition and pressed the starter. As the motor caught, she switched on the lights and surveyed the illuminated dashboard dials. Thank heavens there was plenty of gasoline. The words for "fill it up" and "would you check the air in the left front tire" weren't part of her Spanish vocabulary. She put the car in reverse, maneuvered carefully, and drove out of the lot. Her driving had better be good, she decided grimly, since she didn't know any words for dealing with Spanish policemen either.

As she stopped at an intersection, she looked at her watch in the dashboard light and did some mental arithmetic. According to her calculations, she had about six hours before David would realize what she'd done. Her lips twisted wryly at the thought. Six hours before the egg hit the fan. Sighing softly, she pressed down on the accelerator and concentrated on the winding road.

Gail's first look at Granada in the soft light of dawn told her why the Moors had chosen that location for their famous Alhambra. Protective hills rimmed two sides of the fertile plain which had the river Genil running through it. Even to her travel-weary eyes, the buildings of the modern city nestled effortlessly into their niche at the bottom of the low-lying hills. The endless acres of gray-colored olive trees had given way to the urban dwellings of a contemporary Spanish metropolis to the north and east but the look of old Andalusia still prevailed in the outline of the Alhambra on the crest of a hill to the south.

Rugged limestone walls and dull red-tile roofs hadn't changed since the thirteenth century when Mohammed ben Alhamar had brought river water to the top of the hill and changed the fortification into a paradise of castles and gardens. She recalled the Moorish domination continued until 1492. In the same year Columbus was discovering the New World, his monarchs Ferdinand and Isabella were busily claiming the spectacular Alhambra for their own.

Gail tried to remember the other snippets of information she had read in her guidebook but she was forced to concentrate on her driving. Daylight had brought forth a horde of farmers' carts and trucks and she was kept busy avoiding the loads of produce destined for Granada dinner tables.

At the edge of town, she impulsively turned down a street leading to the railway station. There was a chance that someone had opened the coffee bar for early travelers. She parked near the baggage wagons and made her way to the stand-up bar where a cheerful woman was serving coffee and warm rolls.

"*Café, señorita?*"

164

"Por favor." Gail used two more words from her sparse stock.

The waitress accepted her pesetas without a second glance after she passed over a mug of hot liquid. *"Crema? Azúcar?"*

"No . . . gracias."

The woman shrugged, murmured, *"De nada,"* and went back to reading her newspaper.

The casualness of the transaction made Gail feel better. At least she wouldn't starve to death on her own in Spain even though her diet might be limited. She toyed with the idea of trying for a glass of orange juice in sign language and then decided it was too much trouble. Once she found a hotel, she could order a proper breakfast.

She sipped her scalding coffee carefully as she leaned on the counter and viewed the towering Sierra Nevada peaks behind the foothills. Strange to think of snow-covered mountains complete with ski lifts rimming the sunny Mediterranean. Evidently Spain had a great deal more to offer its visitors than bullfighters and Cordoban leather factories.

Damn! Why had she thought of that? All through the long night of driving, she had kept her mind away from Cordoba and everything that had happened there. Now—just one ill-advised word and David's face flashed up like an unwelcome genie.

She thoughtlessly took a deep swallow of coffee and felt it burn all the way down. Her eyes watered in protest and she wiped them with the back of her hand. Another silly stunt like that and she'd be searching for a hospital instead of a hotel!

She detoured past the station waiting room on her way back to the car and found a rack of advertisements for tourists. After looking at brochures of the various hotels, she found one that looked especially attractive and took the pamphlet with her to an open ticket window. Luckily the railroad clerk knew a little English and a little French so she was able to obtain fairly clear directions on how to get to the hotel.

When she caught sight of the imposing entrance a half hour later, she wondered if she could afford such grandeur for even one day. The branches of the tall shade trees which grew on either side of the cobblestone drive formed a leafy bower at the hotel's elaborate wrought iron gate. Beyond, colorful beds of red and white geraniums led up to the wide front steps of the building. Two gardeners were already watering raised flower boxes by the front door and hosing the patio which contained a separate gift shop.

Since there wasn't a doorman to tell her where to park, Gail merely drew up to the entrance and turned off the engine. At least she wouldn't have far to walk if there weren't any rooms available or if the desk clerk didn't speak English. She crossed her fingers as she went through the front door and headed for the grilled reception section.

She needn't have worried. The hotel clerk's English was fluent enough to have gotten him by anywhere in the world. Before she knew what was happening, he had completed all the formalities and was taking her passport.

"Your room has a splendid view of the city, Miss Alden. Tonight you can watch a fiesta in the town square from your balcony."

Gail shuddered. Balconies again! "I don't think I'll be here for it," she told him carefully. "Actually I want to tour the Alhambra this morning and get a plane to Madrid later in the day."

For the first time he exhibited some concern. "We only have one plane a day to Madrid, Miss Alden. It's very difficult to get reservations on such short notice. However, I will try. . . ."

"Perhaps there's a train. . . ."

166

He shook his head. "The only train to Madrid leaves in about twenty minutes."

"There are buses, I suppose?" Her tone was unenthusiastic.

His, equally so. "I wouldn't recommend them. It's a long ride and the road twists. I have heard Americans do not like the highways in Andalusia." He patted his stomach significantly.

"I see," she said hurriedly before he went into detail about American intestinal weaknesses. "Perhaps I'd better wait and see what you can do about a plane reservation."

His beam reappeared. "Exactly what I'd suggest, Miss Alden. Your room is ready . . . go through the archway ahead and take the first turn to the right." He reached under the counter and produced a big brass key like a magician conjuring a rabbit from a hat. "Our dining room opens in twenty minutes for breakfast service." She started to protest but he held up an authoritative hand. "There is no use going to the Alhambra before nine-thirty . . . that is the official opening time for the palace and the gardens of the Generalife. You'll find more information about the Alhambra in your room." He slapped the key in her hand decisively. "Now . . . is there anything else I can do?"

Gail thought of telling him to apply for a job at the United Nations—that they'd been looking for someone like him to solve their problems for years—but she thought better of it. Instead, she clutched her key and started to move away before she remembered. "Oh, yes. There is one thing . . ." she told him.

He showed surprise but was still polite. "Yes, Miss Alden?"

"My car. . . ."

He waved a manicured hand. "No problem. The boy will get your keys. After he brings in your bags, the car will be parked and locked in our garage behind the hotel. The management accepts full responsibility. . . ."

"You don't understand." She interrupted his conversational tide with difficulty. "I want to give the car away."

His eyebrows climbed.

She was fishing in her purse for her notepad. "But first, I have to tell some people that the car is here so it can be picked up. I don't speak Spanish and I hoped someone in the hotel could make the call for me."

His eyebrows settled down again as he reached for a pen. "That is possible. Who would you like us to call?"

"The residence of a Señor Ricardo Gomez. . . ."

"Gomez is a common name in Spain, Miss Alden. Where does the gentleman live?"

"My word! I don't know." She chewed on the inside of her lip and tried to remember if David had told her. "I *think* he's quite an important person in town. . . ."

"Could you mean the *Conde*?" The clerk was beginning to look impressed.

"I don't know. If it's any help, he's married to a Margarita Gomez and they have a daughter Felipa."

"That is surely the one. I have seen their names in the newspaper many times." He put the pen back in its holder. "If you will go to your room, I will have our operator put the call through immediately."

"But I told you—I don't know any Spanish."

"There is English spoken in that household, Miss Alden." He leaned over the counter confidentially. "Their home is one of the showplaces of Granada. Believe me, it is an honor to have a friend of Señor Gomez staying at our hotel. I, myself, will escort you to your room."

"But I'm not . . . I mean . . . that won't be necessary, thank you." She backed hurriedly from the desk. "Through the archway, you said."

"Just so." He beamed again. "I will have the call put through *inmediatamente*."

She nodded and beat a strategic retreat toward her room. So much for her hopes of an anonymous stay in Granada. She couldn't have attracted more attention to herself if she'd claimed to be a kissing cousin of Generalisimo Franco himself!

Smiling ruefully, she checked her brass key again and then consulted the numbers on the hall doors. Number sixteen must be the next room on the left.

There was barely time for her to enter the high-ceilinged suite when the bedside telephone rang. She went over and lifted the receiver with trembling fingers.

"Hello?"

"Miss Alden?" She recognized the desk clerk's oily tones.

"Speaking."

"Your party is on the wire. Go ahead, please."

"Hello . . . this is Mrs. Gomez." A lovely throaty voice came from the receiver. "Were you calling me?"

Gail gulped. "Margarita Gomez?"

"That's right." The voice lost its impersonal veneer. "Is this Gail?"

"Why, yes!" Amazement made her forget her nervousness. "How did you know about me?"

There was an amused response. "David said you'd probably call. What on earth did you do to my poor brother?"

"Why . . . nothing. He was fine when I left." Fear elevated Gail's voice. "Has something happened to him? He's all right, isn't he?"

"So far as I know." Margarita chuckled. "Except that he's in a terrible temper and ready to flay you alive the next time he sees you."

Gail sighed in relief. "Oh, is *that* all!"

"Isn't it enough?"

"I thought something really bad had happened to him . . . like the trouble in Seville."

"David mentioned that. Until he talked to the desk

169

clerk at the *parador,* he was afraid someone had forced you to leave Cordoba. It's a wonder he didn't call out the police . . . or the army. My brother isn't the most placid soul in the world." She laughed again. "As a matter of fact, neither am I. Short fuses must run in our family." Then, becoming businesslike, "When will you be out to see us?"

"I'm sorry. . . ." Gail was unnerved by her directness. "There won't be time. I hope to get on the Madrid plane later today."

"My dear, that won't do at all. David told me expressly that you'd be staying in Granada."

"I've had to change my plans." Gail didn't want to sound ungrateful but the sooner she severed all connection with the Knight family, the better it would be. "What I really called about was the car . . . David's car. I've parked it here at the hotel. If I leave the keys at the desk, could someone possibly come in and get it? I'd deliver it myself except that. *. . ."* She started to say, "I can't face the possibility of seeing David again," and then realized she couldn't make such a revealing statement to the other woman.

"Except that you won't have time." Margarita finished the sentence for her.

"Er . . . yes."

"All right, Gail." Her voice was brisk but kind. "If that's the way you'd really prefer it. Perhaps we can meet another time."

"I hope so. I'd enjoy returning to Spain."

"Well, I'll be here if you do." There was no disguising the happiness in her simple statement. "My husband has delivered an ultimatum. I must say it's very flattering after all the years we've been married."

"That's wonderful!"

"I think so myself." Laughter bubbled from Margarita's words. "Ricardo's very much like David in issuing ultimatums but in this case, I wish he'd done it months

170

ago. Pippa's beside herself with delight to be home again and that we're all together." She paused. "We'd like so much to meet you, Gail. Are you sure you can't manage it?"

"Honestly, I wish I could," Gail said with real regret. Margarita sounded charming and it would have been fun to meet a sympathetic American woman after so many days abroad. She twisted the telephone cord absently around her finger as she went on, "It's too complicated to explain now. Besides, David will tell you all about it when he comes. He *is* coming, isn't he?"

Margarita was vague. "I believe so. There's no saying exactly when. David hates to be pinned down."

"Probably sooner than you think," Gail advised ominously. She couldn't visualize David calmly sightseeing in Cordoba after all that had happened.

There was a knock on the hall door. It opened part way and a chambermaid poked her head inside.

Gail welcomed the interruption; if the telephone conversation went on much longer, she'd be telling David's sister exactly what happened at the *parador*. That prospect was as chilling as receiving a gift certificate for a visit to the dentist.

"Someone's come in," she told Margarita, "so I must go. It's been wonderful talking to you. . . ."

"But, Gail . . ."

"I'll leave the car keys at the desk under your name. Good-bye, Mrs. Gomez." She put the receiver back on its cradle quickly before she could change her mind.

The maid was backing out the door.

"Did you want something?" Gail asked.

The woman merely pointed to her armful of towels and shook her head, closing the door behind her.

Gail glanced uncertainly about the room. It didn't appear to need any maid service. The furnishings were immaculate from the deep blue velvet-cut rug to the

171

maroon silk draperies on long keyhole windows which overlooked the valley below.

She sighed as she turned back toward the bed. Granada seemed the loveliest place she'd visited yet. What a pity she couldn't stay longer and really enjoy it as Margarita suggested. Not that Margarita would still want to entertain her after she heard last night's episode from David.

Somewhere close by a church bell chimed and she looked at her watch. Just time enough for a bath before breakfast. Once she'd finished eating, she would leave the Mercedes' keys at the desk and walk up the hill to the Alhambra as the clerk suggested.

She went into the modern bathroom with its unusual frescoes worked in the gray- and white-tiled borders and leaned over to turn the taps of the tub. From the hot pipe, the steaming water gushed out. Gail's lips curved in the ghost of a smile. This hotel was certainly worth the tariff. Why then did she suddenly wish she could turn back the clock to a drafty *estalagem* in Portugal?

Fortunately her bout with nostalgia was tempered by a delicious breakfast in the hotel's dining room. The marvelous service and the scent from bouquets of bright red carnations on each table soothed Gail's frayed nerves and made her feel like a well-fed cat who'd discovered a quiet, sunny windowsill. Even the realization that David was probably on a bus nearing Granada didn't alarm her as it had an hour earlier. All she had to do was visit the Alhambra and stay out of his way.

Keeping that strategy in mind, she arranged with her waiter for a box lunch so that she could avoid returning to the hotel at noon. When the food was delivered to her room later, she was charmed to find it packed in a small, square basket that fitted easily over her arm. She tucked a wallet-purse in alongside the picnic fare as
172

well as a folder on the Alhambra. Then, catching up a matching cardigan for her pale yellow dress, she made her way to the lobby.

The car keys were delivered to a gray-haired desk clerk who received her instructions calmly.

"Only for someone from the household of Señora Gomez," he repeated. "Yes, Miss Alden. Is there anything else?"

"No, thank you. I think that's all."

"Shall I say when you will return?"

She shook her head. "No one will be interested." No one being David, of course. And he would be glad to have the woman who slapped his face and then stole his car out of his bailiwick once and for all.

Gail retrieved her lunch basket from the marble counter and said, "I just turn right on the main road and walk up the hill to get to the Alhambra?"

"That's right, Miss Alden. There are English-speaking guides at the ticket office if you want one."

"Thanks, I'll wait and see." She nodded and went out through the wide front door into the sunshine. The sudden glare made her pause on the steps and put on her sunglasses before making her way down the walk to the main roadway.

It felt good to get under the protection of the shade trees when she turned up the hill. She looked overhead at their thick branches, remembering the guidebook had identified them as lime trees and chestnuts. Why should limes and chestnuts sound so much more exotic than maples and oaks at home? Her musing glance noted the shallow ditches on either side of the road where small streams curved and meandered down the hill, the water splashing gently over the worn cobblestones on the way. As she passed a shrubbery thicket, a bright blue bird soared into the air. His shrill call floated back on the humid breeze.

Gail stopped to watch him and catch her breath from

the climb. It was ironic that this Arabic stronghold brought to mind a verse from the New Testament. "Whatsoever things are lovely . . . think on these things," she murmured, admiring the peaceful surroundings. She started on up the hill again, thinking perhaps that it wasn't strange at all.

That morning at the Alhambra provided a glorious jumble of unforgettable sights. There were the magnificent buildings with their exquisite carvings, the Arabic arches with hands symbolizing Mohomet and keys symbolizing faith . . . and everywhere the gardens, their flower beds glazed with hot Spanish sunshine.

The past still lived in the Moorish stronghold. When Gail walked through the harem or the marbled royal baths, she could almost see robed attendants offering sweetmeats or walnut bark for the teeth as they had on other drowsy afternoons.

But if the palace was full of historical beauty, it had its places of tragedy, too. There was the Hall of the Abencerrajes where Boabdil's father murdered all the sons of his first wife. A guide pointed out red stains of iron oxide next to a fountain as indisputable evidence of the gruesome beheadings. Gail shuddered and went on her way, deciding there was something to be said for modern civilization, after all.

By one o'clock, she was surfeit with superlatives and sightseeing. She grasped her lunch basket more tightly and decided to find a secluded spot for her meal. It would give her a chance to digest her picnic and all the wonders she had seen simultaneously.

An amiable guard directed her toward the gardens of the Generalife and she trudged along another shaded walkway. This time she left the formidable palace buildings behind and entered a secluded park that looked as if it were straight from the *Arabian Nights*. Thin cypress trees lined the verge of the path with borders of lilies and roses at their feet. The balmy air

174

that wafted between the tall shrubs bore the scent of the orange and lemon trees beyond.

Her steps moved slower and slower as the cypress gave way to an open area of small gardens . . . each perfect in itself with the inevitable alabaster fountain or marble pool in the center.

In the distance, she could see the strolling figure of a policeman. He was sauntering along, his hands clasped behind his back. Undoubtedly the man was thinking of siesta time like most of his countrymen. Gail glanced at her watch. No wonder the gardens were deserted. She couldn't have picked a better time for her picnic lunch if she'd tried!

She walked over to a marble bench which was partially shaded by a glossy-leaved lemon tree and sat down. There was a small sign edging the rectangular reflection pool in front of her. "No Littering" was proclaimed in four different languages. "Offenders would be jailed and fined" by order of Jorge Santos, *Jefe de la Policia.*

She nodded approvingly. Good for Police Chief Santos! Evidently the Spanish took a strong stand against empty beer bottles and discarded candy wrappers.

The ecology question settled, she turned to the more immediate matter of lunch. She opened her basket and rooted inside, happily emerging with the Iberian version of a Poor Boy sandwich . . . sliced ham and cheese in a long, hard roll. A hard-boiled egg, neatly shelled and wrapped in a cloth napkin, rested in another corner of the basket. Salad and dessert were covered by a large orange and ripe banana.

Gail took a hungry bite of her sandwich and considered the menu. Aside from wishing she could trade the orange for a cup of coffee, the fare couldn't be better. She would even have struggled with the orange except that after trying to eat one daintily, she always needed a complete bath. Imagine the police guard's horror if he

175

found her rinsing her sticky fingers and elbows in the elegant reflection pool. She'd probably be thrown in jail for the rest of the summer!

With that in mind, she took care not to let a single crumb fall on the grass as she finished her sandwich and hard-boiled egg. She peeled the banana and ate it slowly, listening to the thready drone of a tiny insect at her feet. It was the only noise in the warm, lethargic air.

Deliberately she sat up straighter to force sleep away. This was no time to be wanting a nap. She folded the banana peel to tuck it back in her basket. Perhaps if she wrapped it and the orange together in the napkin. . . .

"So this is where you've got to! Man . . . you're hard to find." The masculine voice came from behind her to shatter the stillness.

She turned in surprise, still clutching the remnants of her lunch. "Stan! I didn't hear you coming. . . ."

"That's because you were a million miles away." He sat down on the bench beside her and took out a handkerchief to wipe his forehead. "My God, it's hot! Why didn't you come back to the hotel for lunch like a civilized person?"

"Is that a mark of civilization?"

"Certainly . . . at these temperatures." He pulled his sport shirt away from his body and flapped the tail of it like a fan. "Just like the air in a cross-town subway."

She smiled. "Maybe . . . but there's quite a difference in the smell." Inwardly she was wishing that he'd move on and let her recapture the solitude.

"Who cares about that? Y'know, I've been through every building on the top of this hill looking for you."

"What for?" Belatedly, she realized her bald statement was scarcely flattering. "I mean—did you want me for something special?"

"I sure did." He reached for her hands and found

176

himself clutching the moist end of a banana peel. "What the devil!"

"Oh, I'm sorry." She couldn't help laughing at his chagrin. "Remnants of lunch," she explained. "I was just finishing when you came."

He wiped his hand on his handkerchief, still irritated. "There's no need to keep clutching it. Why don't you get rid of the garbage?"

She started to explain about the litter sign and decided it was too much trouble. "Any minute now," she promised blithely. Then, "How did you know where to look for me?"

"The bellboy told me you were headed for the Alhambra. I thought I'd better find you before Knight started taking you to pieces. You should have seen him steaming at the *parador* last night when he discovered you'd already taken off."

"He knew last night?"

"Sure he did. I thought I was the only one in the place with insomnia but I guessed wrong. He was stomping around the lobby most of the night."

She wanted to hear more but was almost afraid to ask. "Was he really mad?"

"Whoo-ee . . . was he!" Stan had evidently forgotten about shaking hands with the slimy banana peel. "What did you do to the guy—make off with his bankroll?"

Gail took refuge in dignity. "I don't know what you mean."

"The devil you don't. Never mind. I *can* tell you this, though. If you want to make points with a man . . . next time don't steal his car." His shoulders shook with laughter. "Knight had to wake up every garage keeper in Cordoba to find another one."

"Did he?"

"Did he what?"

"Find another car?"

"I suppose so . . . eventually." He shrugged. "I didn't stay around to find out."

She almost asked why he didn't offer David a ride and then decided it wasn't a good idea. Stan wasn't the type for generous impulses.

". . . so I checked out the likely hotels here in town," he was saying, "and finally hit pay dirt. That's when I came looking for you."

"If I'd known my movements were so important, I'd have left a paper trail," she said wryly.

"Don't be like that, sweetie. I told you I'd be around." He got to his feet and mopped his forehead again. "I hope you've had enough of this place. Let's take off."

She stared up at him, bewildered. "What are you talking about? I'm sorry—but you'll have to clue me in."

"There's a special eating place on the edge of town. Not too many tourists know about it . . . and they do a *paella* that's out of this world. We can stop at another place I know for a drink, first. You don't mind if we take your car, do you? I left mine downtown for servicing."

"Hey . . . wait a minute. You're going too fast for me." She smiled to soften the blow before she said, "I can't make any dates for the evening because I'm planning to be on the plane to Madrid."

"There's lots of time for a drive now. We can decide about dinner later."

She shook her head helplessly. "You don't understand. I can't take the car out again. For one thing, it belongs to David. And for another, I've already called his sister and asked her to pick it up. I told the clerk at the hotel."

His face settled in grim lines. "That's what he said."

"Well, then." Suddenly she frowned. "You've already asked the clerk? Whatever for?"

178

"When it comes to catching on to things, you aren't the brightest, Gail." He bent over and put a forceful hand under her elbow. "I hoped we could do this in a nice and easy way. C'mon."

She stood up but remained firm when he would have urged her down the path.

"I wish you'd stop being cryptic and"—she jerked her arm to dislodge his grip—"let go of me. I *told* you that I'd made other plans. If that inconveniences you, I'm sorry."

"My God, you still aren't with it!" His fleshy hand dug into her forearm. "I don't give a damn about your plans . . . I want that car of yours."

"But it's David's . . . or at least he rented it. Actually it belongs to a garage in Lisbon."

"Jeez!" He struck his forehead with his free hand. "Do you want me to draw you a picture? I know all about the car."

Comprehension made her mouth drop open in surprise. She closed it quickly at his derisive smirk.

"Then you knew about Josef too, didn't you?" Her words came out slowly. "You've known about him all along."

He shot an impatient look at his watch. "If you're hoping for a hearts and flowers confession, you've got the wrong pigeon. Right now I intend to look through the Mercedes and it'll be easier to get it from that stinking hotel garage if you come and claim the keys." He yanked her alongside of him. "Let's walk back down the hill nice and easy."

"Go fly a kite," she told him, digging her heels into the path. "If you don't let go of me this instant, I'll scream my head off."

His jaw jutted. "Who the hell do you think's going to hear you?"

"That park policeman if nobody else." There was a surge of triumph in her voice as she nodded toward the end of the garden where the uniformed constable strolled down the path.

"Get this straight, doll! If you so much as open your mouth to breathe you'll be damned sorry." Stan gritted the words out and his vicious grip made her gasp with pain. "Make any noise and you'll spend the rest of the month in a hospital ward. Get it?" He waited for her jerky nod before adding, "Stay beside me and keep your mouth shut. Once we get to the hotel, tell the clerk you've changed your mind and that you want the car keys so you can go for a drive." He increased the pressure on her arm, seemingly enjoying her involuntary moan. "Understand?"

Her breath came fast. "You've made your point . . . there's no need to break my arm!"

The pressure eased slightly. "I hope you have a good memory."

"It's great." Her tone was tremulous but still defiant. "I remember what happened to Josef."

"That's good. It *could* happen to you. Don't get any ideas about that being a confession, though. Viv and I have perfect alibis—we were with you when Josef tried to chisel a bigger share. That greedy bastard's lucky to still be alive." He urged her forward. "Let's go. You can read all the details in your morning newspaper."

"Wait a minute," she protested. "I have to get rid of this stuff in my hands. . . . I can't go into the hotel carrying banana peels and oranges. . . ."

"Well then, for God's sake . . . get rid of them," he ordered angrily. "Right now!"

"Whatever you say." Meekly she tossed them over her shoulder.

There was a resounding splash as the orange hit the middle of the reflection pool and another splash as the banana peel landed beside it.

Then all hell broke loose!

There was a shriek of the policeman's whistle—

followed by a volley of angrily shouted Spanish—followed by the pounding of the officer's feet as he tore across the garden toward them.

Stan's head swiveled. "What's going on? Why you damned little . . ." The rest of the exclamation was lost in the confusion. He looked around desperately, weighing his chances. Then he dropped her arm and broke into a run for the far side of the garden.

"Stop!" Gail shouted, taking off after him. "Come back here, you crook!"

The policeman's whistle shrilled again. From behind, came a loud angry shout: *"Deténgase! Deténgase! Ahora mismo, señorita!"*

Gail didn't know what the first words meant but the last one meant he was definitely talking to her and from the outraged roar in his voice he wasn't welcoming her to Granada.

Slithering to a stop, she turned to face him. "For pete's sake, can't you get it straight? It wasn't my fault. I threw that stuff deliberately to get your attention. Stop that man who's running away!"

The officer panted up the path, still waving his arms. *"En Español, por favor, señorita. . . ."*

"I don't *speak* Spanish. Oh, for the love of heaven . . . doesn't anybody in this place speak English?"

"I do. But don't bother to call me . . . I'll call you," said a third voice.

Gail whirled to see a familiar figure strolling up a side path toward her.

Because she'd had a horrible ten minutes and she wasn't out of trouble yet, tears coursed down Gail's cheeks as she threw herself across the intervening yards and wound her arms tightly around a stubborn, but beloved neck. "David! Thank God . . . is it really you?"

And because he'd had no sleep the night before and was feeling like a pool of melted butter after climbing the Alhambra hill in the broiling sun, David merely suffered her embrace and growled, "Of course, it's me. Who the devil were you expecting . . . Don Quixote?"

She giggled helplessly as reaction set in. "I suppose he sent his best."

"From another windmill. You've been busy in your spare time." He glanced over her shoulder at the policeman who looked ready to explode at this new interruption.

She nodded urgently. "It's a terrible mix-up. I just threw that garbage in the pond to get his attention when Stan tried to make me go with him. You have to tell the officer that Stan is the one he wants . . . and probably he's halfway to the Mercedes by now."

"Relax. Stan's on his way for questioning instead. He ran right into a couple of policemen when he cut through the shrubbery. I'll explain it later—you're the one who's in the soup at the moment."

"I know," she wailed. "David, he looks as if he means to throw me in jail. Can you raise bail or something?"

"Of course." His reassuring voice was silky. "I'll do my best to arrange it during visiting hours. Let me see what I can do." He turned to address the policeman in rapid Spanish.

The loud tirade answering him was accompanied by a series of threatening gestures and scowls which made Gail shrink still closer to David's side. When it finally tapered off, she tugged at her protector's elbow. "Tell me! What did he say? When are the visiting hours?"

David bent his head—his eyes kindling with unholy glee. "Sorry about this, darling. They're from noon till three P.M."

"That's all right. . . ."

He interrupted sadly. "Starting one week from today."

CHAPTER NINE

"I don't know why I even bother to talk to you," Gail said. "Anybody who has a fiendish sense of humor like yours should be abandoned on a desert island with the other nuts."

She was addressing David's recumbent form three hours later as they watched a waiter deposit two frosty glasses of gin and tonic on the balcony table of her hotel room.

David merely opened one eye and commanded, "Please sign the check, Miss Alden." He continued loftily. "I'll deduct seventy-five cents from your bail bond."

She did as he asked and tipped the waiter as he bowed his way out. Turning back to David, who was once again snoozing comfortably in the big upholstered chair, she said, "Make it a dollar even. You forgot the tip."

He pretended to consider it. "All right—but just this once. From now on, gratuities are on you."

"In that case, I hope the waiter understood English."

"So do I. He'll enjoy telling the rest of the staff that they have a jailbird . . . or should I say parolee . . . roosting in this room."

She glared at him. "Calling you a sadist wasn't bad enough! You're a . . . a . . ."

"Give up, angel." He did open his eyes then and his grin flashed. "You know you're dying to learn what happened. Come over here"—he patted the arm of his chair invitingly—"and I'll tell you all about it."

She moved forward warily.

David leaned back. "If you'd bring my drink, then I wouldn't have to exert myself. Cut that out! You miserable maggot! How dare you waste good gin by pouring it on a man's head!" He brushed off the few drops trickling down his forehead and tried to look severe. "The first thing a nursemaid must learn is to watch her language."

"Not the first thing," she said, perching on the arm of his chair. "Not if they work for you. I should have poured the whole drink over you—letting me sit in that jail for two and a half hours!"

"You weren't in jail. . . ."

"Well, the anteroom, then. . . ."

"The captain's office," he corrected, "and his furniture was better than this. Anyhow, it served you right. You had time to think over your sins."

"Hah! I'll bet you dragged your feet on purpose. Imagine telling a woman that visiting day wasn't for one whole week. . . ."

"You deserved that, too," he informed her complacently. "They only had you up for littering. I could have changed the charge to Grand Theft—Auto." Her suddenly embarrassed expression made him backtrack. "Hey, if you're going to take me seriously it's no fun."

She concentrated on the fabric of the chair. "You were serious last night at the *parador*. That's how the trouble started."

"I know." His face sobered and he caught her hand to hold it against his cheek. "Now I'm serious about something else. I'm marrying you just as soon as it can be arranged, sweetheart. Margarita's planning the festivities and Ricardo's cutting the red tape."

184

Her eyes dimmed with tears. "David, you fool!" she protested gently. "You're supposed to ask the woman to say 'yes.' "

"You've said 'yes' in a dozen different ways ever since I found you waiting in that Paris hotel lobby and I was telling you that I loved you all over Portugal and Spain." He turned his lips to brush her palm. "You know that's true."

She would have liked to surrender completely but a vestige of pride remained. "I can think of one town where you didn't."

"So can I," he said with a wry twist to his mouth. "I made a mistake in Cordoba. . . . I knew it thirty seconds after I finished polishing the floor with you. If you want an explanation, I can only admit that I was a damned fool . . . and a jealous one. That torn dress of yours made me want to murder somebody and since I was too late for Donnell, you got the brunt of it." His glance held hers frankly. "You'll note that I'm just apologizing for what I said . . . not what I did."

Her cheeks flamed at that. "As long as you're being so generous—I'd better apologize, too. There wasn't any excuse for my slapping you. I felt terrible afterward."

"Forget it. Now—if everything's settled, you can stop being so elusive." He put his drink on the floor and deposited hers beside it. "Come here," he ordered, pulling her down from her perch and across his lap.

"Wait! You're going too fast," she protested.

"What makes you think so? It's taken me three years to get this far." He bent his head and kissed her hungrily.

It was clear that he was wasting no more time.

She pushed him away finally. "Let me get my breath. . . ."

David was having trouble with his own respiration.

"You *are* marrying me, aren't you?" he persisted doggedly.

"I really think I'd better." Then, "Darling, you know I will."

"Thank God! You had me worried there for a while." He pulled her closer. "Where were we?"

"No!" She captured his hand and held it firmly. "We're just engaged . . . not married."

"It's going to be a very short engagement."

"At least long enough to tell me what's happened," she insisted.

"Wouldn't you rather know what's going to happen?" He grinned and bent to whisper in her ear.

By the end of his first sentence, her cheeks were fiery. She drew herself upright. "Maybe we should have a long engagement."

"Okay . . . you win." He was still laughing at her. "What do you want to know?"

"What's happened to Josef . . . for one thing?"

He reached down beside the chair and handed her drink to her and retrieved his own before answering. "Protection," he told her solemnly. After a swallow, "Josef's coming along nicely. The police finally put on enough pressure that he told where he'd hid the Goncalves painting. That's the reason we all converged on you today."

It was hard to hold a rational conversation perched on David's knees, but Gail tried. "Since Stan made all the fuss about the Mercedes, I suppose it was somewhere in the car."

David must have been aware of the tremulous undercurrents. He grinned mockingly again. "You suppose right. Josef really excelled this time. He had it neatly sandwiched between protective coverings in the sunshine top."

Her eyes widened. "I'll be darned! The roof panel with the broken catch . . . at least, that's what he said."

186

"So, of course, we didn't try it." He sipped his drink. "From what the police say, the rest of his pals didn't think he actually had it with him. But they kept nudging him—to remind him that they were waiting for the scheduled delivery. That was the reason for the close miss in Obidos."

"Wasn't that a relative of Pippa's nurse?"

"We thought it was. Probably Josef knew differently all along. No wonder he was so shaken that night. He'd planned to go directly to Spain from Lisbon and the first thing I did was change the itinerary to make him hang around in Portugal another day. It gave his cohorts a chance to catch up with him."

"Plus another day to watch over his car."

David traced a star on her forehead. "Go to the head of the class."

"It's about time. I certainly didn't know what was going on then."

"Probably because you were so overwhelmed with my personality," he said modestly.

"Hah! You were still biting my head off at that point."

"Not then. Earlier . . . yes. Next time you flirt with a French tourist I'll do more than that."

"Look who's talking. When I remember how you acted with Vivian . . ." Her eyebrows went up suddenly. "Vivian! What about Vivian?"

"That's my girl. Slow but steady."

She pursed her lips. "About that long engagement of ours. . . ."

"Okay, okay. I surrender," he said, responding promptly. "Vivian disappeared from the scene after Seville." His eyes crinkled at the corners. "And now I can add blackmail to your lengthy criminal record."

She smiled. "So sue me. According to Stan, Vivian was visiting friends in Cordoba."

"I doubt it. Vivian was part of the window dressing.

After Seville, she wasn't needed. The police should discover her whereabouts this afternoon."

"I don't think they'll get much from Stan," she hazarded. "At least, not from the way he was talking in the garden. Naturally he'd try to protect his sister."

"Naturally. If she *were* his sister," David agreed. "Did she look like a sister to you?"

Gail shook her head slowly.

"Nor to me—but I have a nasty suspicious mind." He held up his hand as she would have spoken. "Don't you say a word!"

She laughed and reached over to smooth a piece of his hair which was poking straight up. Naturally David had to thank her properly for such attention. After a short but highly satisfactory interval, he went on, "The police can certainly find out if Stan and Vivian are related. As far as making criminal charges stick, that's a matter for the lawyers. Josef is the key prosecution witness and apparently he didn't know the Donnells . . . or whatever their real names are . . . until he learned in Seville."

"Then you think they turned up at Obidos to watch Josef?"

"That's the general belief. I suppose they were watching us, too." He swirled the ice in his glass thoughtfully. "We *could* have been in the double cross with Josef."

"I suppose so. They must have searched your luggage in Faro . . . since they knew we'd be there." She frowned intently. "I'll bet that cleaning man in Seville was planning to do the same thing in my hotel room. No wonder he was startled when I appeared—he probably thought I'd gone out with you and Josef that afternoon."

"Hold it!" David clamped onto her shoulder. "What's all this about a cleaner in Seville? It's the first I've heard of it."

188

"Nothing important, darling." She gave him a capsule version of that afternoon's happenings and finished by saying, "I didn't mention it to you before dinner because I thought I was just imagining things. Then, after Josef's accident, it completely slipped my mind." She sighed. "All that night at Obidos, I was blaming everything on your poor brother-in-law."

"And Ricardo was just doing his darnedest to pull his marriage back together again. He knew the only way he could get Margarita over here was to keep Pippa beyond the legal visiting time. He was right, of course. Margarita was so flaming mad that she forgot she wasn't speaking to him except through her lawyers."

"But everything's all right now, isn't it?"

"Right as rain," he confirmed.

"From the way your sister sounded this morning, I gathered it was."

He dropped a light kiss on her eyebrow. "She was afraid to say very much for fear you'd take off again and be harder to find next time. I'd already told her about my intentions for you, madam."

"Was *that* why she was so evasive when I asked if you were on the way?"

"Sure. Margarita's all for happy endings these days." He glanced at his watch. "We'd better get moving pretty soon. I told her we'd be there in plenty of time for dinner. There are lots of things to settle. . . ."

"Just a darned minute." She pushed him back. "You haven't said a thing about what's going to happen to me."

"You mean, you *still* don't know? I must be losing my touch," he decided. "Or maybe you just need more convincing."

"I'm talking about my trouble with the police, you dope." At his amused look, she added, "As you well know."

He merely grinned.

"Well, what happens now?" she persisted. "Am I on parole?"

"You could say that. The police were willing to listen when I said I'd be responsible for you. . . ."

"David! Stop fudging."

"All right, my master criminal. They were happy to see the back of you when I assured them you didn't know anything about the Goncalves painting and that you'd driven the Mercedes here with my approval."

"Some approval!" she said with feeling.

"Naturally there'll be an extra charge later on since I had to commit perjury."

"I can imagine."

"But I figured it wouldn't be much of a honeymoon with the bride in jail. . . ."

"Since the visiting hours didn't start until a week from today," she intoned.

"Precisely. So I decided—what's a little perjury between friends? It was easier for the police chief too; he's a good friend of Ricardo and he'll undoubtedly be invited to the wedding."

"For her going-away outfit, the bride wore stripes," she murmured. "Did I get off scot-free on the littering charge, too?"

"Finally. That was the worst of all. For God's sake, don't sling any more banana peels around while we're here."

"I just did it to try and attract the officer's attention."

"I know, dearest." He patted her shoulder soothingly. "You know, threatening you is one charge Stan Donnell will find hard to beat."

She shuddered at the memory. "I wonder if he really would have hurt me?"

"He needed your help to get possession of the car. There was a lot of money involved and his people didn't care how they achieved their results." David's face grew bleak. "When you think what happened to Josef. . . ."

"Don't think of it," she commanded. "I'm not going to. Not when there are so many nice things in the offing." Her voice was dreamy. "Whoever would have believed there would be such a lovely ending when I answered that ad in Paris?"

He took her empty glass and put it on the floor beside his. "Discreet young woman with highest morals," he quoted. "I certainly was snagged by my own bait," he added comfortably.

"Well, I like that!"

"Mmmm. So do I." He pulled her head back down on his shoulder. "Some morals! You almost got us reported for indecent exposure in Obidos . . . you stole my car and deserted me without notice in Cordoba"— she wriggled but he held her tightly—"and you're picked up as a public nuisance in Granada. You make an innocent man commit perjury and reward him by running off with his heart. . . ."

"And his love?" she questioned softly.

"Every bit of it. Now . . . always." His eyes questioned her. "For you, too?"

"Oh, yes!" She sighed happily. "I guess I'll have to confess—you're dealing with a habitual criminal. There's nothing for it but a life sentence." Then she couldn't prolong the teasing any longer. She leaned forward. "Darling David. I do love you so much."

Her lips feathered down his lean cheek until he turned his head with a muffled groan and caught her in a hard, possessive kiss.

She was aware of the warmth of his hand on her back through the thin material of her dress—she felt it move to pull her even closer—and then everything blurred in the delight of love's fulfillment.

It was considerably later when David murmured something close to her ear.

"What did you say, darling?" she asked like a sleepy kitten.

His grin was slow, triumphant. "Nothing important. Just that we'd better call Margarita and tell her we'll be late for dinner."